The Nightmare Man

JG Faherty

Lycan Valley Press Publications
1002 N Meridian STE 100-153
Puyallup, Washington 98371 United States of America

Printed in the United States of America

First Edition

ISBN-13: 978-1-64562-021-1

Duérmete niño, duérmete ya...
Que viene el Cuco y te comerá.

(Sleep child, sleep now...
Or else El Cuco will come and eat you)

—Traditional Spanish Lullaby

CHAPTER ONE

6 YEARS AGO...

KENJI YAMADA PEERED into the dark hallway, his heart pounding so hard he heard it in his head. The only light came from the stars and moon outside. *Torihada* covered his arms, what his American friends called goosebumps. The floor was ice against his bare feet, adding to his chills. He shivered, but not from the cold.

In his right hand, the *sujihiki* knife he'd taken from the kitchen threatened to slip free from his sweaty fingers.

Holding his breath, Kenji eased down the hall to the bathroom. He reached for the handle and paused.

Why was the door open a few inches? Hadn't he shut it when he left to hide?

He tried to remember, but the *thump-thump-thump* in his head made it hard to think.

Stop being a baby. Toshio and his friends play this all the time.

Before he could change his mind, Kenji pushed the door open and jumped into the bathroom, the knife thrust forward.

"Odoroki! Watashi wa Teddy o hakken!"

Except the surprise was on him. The teddy bear no longer stared up from the water in the bathtub.

Tiny puddles led from the tub across the tile into the hall. His feet were so cold he hadn't noticed the wet floor. Gripping the knife in both hands, he followed the damp spots to his own bedroom. The light was a little brighter in there because of the glowing stars painted on his ceiling. A whispering, slithering sound came from under the bed. Biting his lip, Kenji knelt down and peered into the dark space.

Two red, glowing eyes stared back at him.

"Ah!" He jabbed the knife forward. The sharp blade pierced something thick but soft. When he withdrew his arm, his soaking wet teddy bear came with it, impaled on the knife.

"Watashi wa Teddy o hakken," Kinji whispered, following the rules of the game. You had to tell the bear you found it, or else the *oni*, the demon, would keep trying to hide.

Teddy remained motionless as Kenji carried it back to the bathroom, its ordinary brown plastic eyes refusing to give away any secrets as to how it had traveled to the bedroom.

Kenji dropped it in the tub, still impaled on the

knife.

"Anata wa onidesu," he said in a loud voice, and then hurried from the room. Now that he'd told the oni to come seek him, it was his turn to hide. He ran to the kitchen, where he'd already prepared a spot at the bottom of the pantry. His glass of salt water waited there, along with a piece of candy in case he got hungry waiting for sunrise. The space was tight, but he squeezed in and pulled the door shut. Slats in the thin wood provided tiny gaps through which the table and chairs were visible as indistinct, ghostly shapes in the darkness.

As the minutes dragged on, Kenji's breathing slowed and his heart no longer beat like a *talko* drum. He found himself wishing he'd brought his phone with him, or his watch. Time moved slower than normal in the dark, cramped space, and soon had no idea how long he'd been hiding. Ten minutes? Twenty?

Something *thumped* at the other end of the house. Followed by the *clink* of metal on tile.

Kenji's heart sped up again. A picture formed in his head, Teddy dropping from the edge of the tub to the floor, knife in one furry paw. The air grew heavy, making it hard to breathe. The darkness no longer seemed mysterious, it seemed... sinister, a word he'd learned from Toshio. It meant there was danger nearby but you couldn't see it, you could only feel it. He'd laughed at his brother, saying you couldn't feel danger.

He'd been wrong.

More sounds, soft and fast. Like fingers tapping on a table. *Or a small animal running through the house.*

Kenji shivered. Had the room grown colder or was it just his fear? More pitter-pattering, this time in the hallway. Coming closer.

In the family room, the television turned on.

Game show contestants shouted for prizes, their voices unnaturally loud in the empty house. Blue, flickering light seeped into the kitchen, and now Kenji could see the table and chairs in front of him, blocking his view of the hall.

He noticed his breath making clouds of steam in the frigid air. Afraid it might give him away, he put a hand over his mouth and turned his head.

A sudden thought came to him. With the TV volume so high, he wouldn't hear Teddy coming for him.

That's what it wants.

Something moved in the kitchen, a low, gray shape that passed by too fast for Kenji to make out the features. He knew, though. *Teddy.* Searching for him.

Right then, he wished he'd never decided to play the game, wished he'd never heard Toshio and his friends talking about *Hitori Kakurenbo*. A game of hide and seek with a demon. *"It's not real, stupid,"* Toshio had said when Kenji asked why they'd do something so dangerous. *"It's just a way to have fun when no one is home."*

Of course, no one ever left Kenji home alone. He was too young. So he'd forgotten about the game.

Until tonight.

Their parents were visiting friends for the evening, and they'd left Toshio to babysit. But he'd snuck out when he thought Ken was asleep. That's when Ken decided to play the game, like the older kids.

But now it didn't seem so fun.

I wish I'd stayed asleep.

Something banged, making Kenji jump and gasp. His salt water spilled on his lap.

The back door opening?

"Ima sugu anata no heya ni iki, Toshio!"

His mother's voice, ordering Toshio to go to his room?

His parents were home! His brother's legs went past the door, sneakered feet stomping hard. The kitchen door shut and car keys jangled as they landed on the counter.

Ha! Toshio is in trouble for leaving me alone and I'm safe now. Kenji reached up for the door handle.

And froze as Toshio screamed.

At that moment, Kenji realized his mistake.

No one knew he was playing *Hitori Kakurenbo*! That meant they weren't expecting the *oni* to be there.

Toshio cried out again, only this time the sound ended in mid-shout. Kenji's mother and father called out to him and ran to find him. Kenji wanted to yell, to warn them, but his mouth refused to move, frozen like the rest of his body.

A terrible roar shook the thin walls of the house. More screams followed. Something crashed. There were other sounds: the *crunch* and *crack* of wood breaking, glass shattering, things hitting the floor. Thunderous footsteps pounded up and down the hall, in and out of rooms. The lights went out, plunging the house back into near darkness. At one point, a giant shadow moved past the pantry, black against the gray. A terrible odor filled the room, the stink of rotten food and farts and sewers mixed together.

Kenji clutched his half-empty glass of salt water and held his breath as two red lights appeared outside the pantry door, accompanied by heavy breathing. They dipped down and moved closer, close enough for him to see they weren't lights, *they were eyes,* giant red eyes with sideways pupils like a goat's.

Then they rose up again and the *oni* moved away, the heavy footsteps vibrating the floor.

Soon after, the house grew silent again.

A desire grew inside Kenji, a desire to open the closet and peek at the clock over the stove, but he forced it down. He could still feel danger in the air. Besides, that wasn't how the game was played.

Not if you wanted to live.

So he waited, tears ice cold on his cheeks,

choking back the sobs that wanted to burst free.

He was still in the pantry when the police arrived, long after the morning sun filled the kitchen. By then, he knew it was safe to come out. He just couldn't make himself do it. Something awful waited out there. And it was all his fault.

He hadn't followed the rules; now his family was dead.

And the oni was free.

CHAPTER TWO

PRESENT DAY...

IT WAS AFTER midnight, and Talia Greer was wide awake.

She'd pretended to go to sleep earlier, when her father tucked her in. After he went downstairs, she'd gone under the covers with a flashlight and the Maya Blair mystery book she'd started reading after school. It was so good she couldn't turn the pages fast enough, and then all of a sudden it was done and her heart was thumping like she'd run a race in gym class.

Now she was too excited to fall asleep. She couldn't stop thinking about Maya and Lucy and wishing she could have adventures like they did.

Her mother would be so mad if they knew she'd been reading a ghost story at night.

"Those books will give you nightmares!"

But it never happened, because Talia knew the difference between made up stories and real life.

Monsters and ghosts only existed in books and movies. Despite what some of the kids in her class believed. Like Ryan Holland, who said he'd seen the boogem-man the other night.

"It's called the boogeyman, stupid," she'd told him. Everyone had laughed. "And it's not real."

"Is so," he'd insisted. "I saw it. Right outside my window. Bigger than Coach Fogarty and it had red eyes."

"You're lying." Talia pointed at him and the other kids went *Ooooh.* "Nobody's bigger than Mr. Fogarty. You were just dreaming and got scared like a baby."

"Ryan's a baby!" someone shouted, and several voices joined in. "Baby! Baby! Ryan is a baby."

Ryan had started crying, which made everyone tease him more.

But Talia was no baby. Which was why the different noises of the house at night didn't bother her as she lay inside her pretend tent. Her daddy had explained it to her.

"Wood changes shape as the temperature gets warmer or colder. When it does that, it makes noise. We call it settling."

Talia knew all the noises their house made at night. The *groan* of wood settling. The *clink-clunk* of ice cubes dropping in the freezer. The soft *tick-tick-tick* of the clock over the fireplace. The *hummm* of the air conditioning turning on.

Creak.

Talia frowned. She knew that one, too. It was the

sound the floor made when someone stood by the door. Except how could that be? No one was there. Or were they? Had her father snuck down the hall to make sure she was asleep?

Was she about to get in trouble?

She clicked the flashlight off and held her breath.

Creak.

A picture came to her. A ghost, one that looked a lot like the spirit of the old pirate Maya and Lucy had been fighting. Standing at the foot of her bed. Staring at her. Watching her, and not in a good way. In a creepy way, like it wanted to hurt her.

Creak.

"Dad?" The word popped out of her mouth before she could stop it. Now he knew she was awake!

Nothing happened. Slowly, she pulled the comforter down. Nobody was there.

Just the house settling. Don't be a baby.

She closed her eyes. She really did need to get to sleep or she'd be tired and cranky for school in the morning.

A nasty odor filled her nose. It reminded her of the time the bathroom toilets overflowed at school. Warm air blew on her cheeks, as if someone was breathing on her from only inches away. She opened her eyes, expecting to see her father there after all.

A horrible face stared at her, covered in thick fur like a caveman. Giant red eyes glowed in the dark. The creature opened its mouth and growled, showing big, sharp teeth.

Talia had time for one thought before giant claws grabbed her.

Ryan Holland hadn't lied.

Detective Rob Navarro's stomach clenched as he approached the body. The young boy's eyes stared at him in silent reproach.

You did this to me.

For a moment, the scene wavered, a second image overlaying the corpse. A different boy, with darker skin, his hands wrapped around a rubber ball.

You killed me.

No. Rob closed his eyes, took a deep breath. Opened them again. Only one body. The other boy was gone, at least for now. He'd come back again, though. Either in his dreams or while Rob studied the crime scene photos. Despite what his psychiatrist said, he knew the boy would haunt him forever.

And maybe he deserved it.

Focus. You've got a job to do.

He crouched down near the body, careful to avoid the red splatters painting the walls and floor. More blood drenched the bedsheets. The crime scene unit had already finished their preliminary work, taking photographs, scraping under the victim's fingernails, swabbing blood samples. Now it was his turn.

Danny Mitchell, age twelve. Killed while the family slept. Just like the last one. Clothes in tatters, flesh shredded beneath them. Arms and legs bent into shapes they were never intended to make.

Pretty much everything in between them missing, the chest and belly split open and emptied, naked ribs protruding from ragged flesh. Like a giant mouth filled with fangs, silently mocking his futile efforts to bring the killer to justice.

You'll never find me. I could be anyone. A stranger in town. Someone you know. Maybe even a neighbor.

So far, they'd only found traces of evidence at the other scenes. A few odd hairs that hinted the killer may have worn a fur coat or hat. Some saliva, but the DNA wasn't salvageable. The lab hadn't matched the wounds to any known weapon. Even the experts in Manhattan and Washington were baffled. One of them suggested it looked like wild animals had scavenged the body.

Rob's guilt rose up again, only this time without the ghosts from his past to deliver it.

Maybe I didn't kill him, but in a way, it's my fault. Three kids missing and now two dead. And I have no idea how to stop it.

He eyed the room. The parents hadn't heard anything until his screams woke them. When they got to the room, it was empty except for their dead son. No signs of forced entry and the doors to the house were still locked from the inside. The upstairs windows were open to let in the mild September air, but all the screens were firmly in place, and no ladder marks outside.

The heartbreaking sound of weeping reached him from outside. The rest of the Mitchell family waited in the driveway while the police conducted their investigation. Sooner rather than later, he'd have to speak to them, before the shock fully wore off and their awful grief ravaged them as viciously as the monster that killed their son. It was part of his job, even though all he wanted to do was go home and wrap his arms around his own children, keep them safe forever.

Except no one was ever safe. He'd learned that the night of his eighth birthday, when the spectre of death appeared at his window.

Red eyes glowing through the screen. The face of the demon gazing at him. The stench of the beast...

Cuco!

His eyes went to Danny's mangled body again. Was it possible...?

No. That was just a childhood fantasy. A nightmare, the first of many but still nothing more than that. A child's reaction to the murders haunting the city that summer.

Don't let guilt and fear rule you.

Easier said than done. It was hard to forget the monsters.

Especially when you were one.

Rob arrived home just as Allison slid dinner out of the oven. The enticing aromas of baked chicken, herbed rice, and string beans met him at the door. His body reacted in Pavlovian fashion, his stomach immediately growling and his mouth filling with saliva despite his gruesome day.

"You're late," Allison said, giving him a peck on the cheek while simultaneously sprinkling powdered garlic on the beans.

"Yeah." The last thing he wanted was to talk about work. He tried his best to keep the gloom of his job out of the house, for his family's sake and his own sanity. But it wasn't like the Mitchell boy's death was a secret. The story made the local news channels within hours, and thanks to the internet, most people probably knew about it before that. By now there'd be a thousand theories making their way across Rocky Point.

"The captain called a special meeting. Until this lunatic is caught, everyone is basically on call twenty-four seven."

"And that's different how?" Allison gave him a wry smile as she handed him dishes to put on the table. As one of only three detectives on the Rocky Point police force, he often got called to crime scenes at all hours of the day or night. Something you never got used to as a cop's wife, but you accepted.

Rob shrugged. "Normally I'd be happy for the overtime, but all I want is to see this bastard behind bars. There's talk about implementing a mandatory curfew. The mayor and the board are meeting about it tomorrow."

"That reminds me." Allison took the chicken from the oven and set it on the stove. "Heather got invited to a sleepover at Chrissy George's house on Saturday."

"I don't know if that's a good idea. Not right now."

"She's sixteen. And she'll be just as safe there as here, you know that."

Rob couldn't deny it. Fred George had been a New York City cop for twelve years, until he busted his ankle in a car accident and went out on permanent disability. Now he worked as a car salesman, but he still had his guns and knew how to use them if he had to.

None of which made Rob feel better. Before he could object again, Allison poked a finger in his chest.

"A little bird told me there's a good chance Ken will get invited, too. Which means we'll have the house to ourselves."

Both kids gone? He and Allison hadn't had a whole night alone in forever. Since adopting Ken six months earlier, they'd been doing everything as a family in order to help their new son adjust. Between that and his long hours at work, there'd hardly been time to just be husband and wife.

I owe her this.

"Okay. Tell her she can go. And Ken, too." He grabbed her by the waist and kissed her.

"I'm sure we can think of something to do with the time."

CHAPTER THREE

"DADDY, HELP!"

Rob Navarro opened his eyes to pure darkness. His daughter's terrified cries echoed through the house. He leaped out of bed and struck his hip against a piece of furniture that shouldn't be there. Disorientation sent him stumbling into a wall he couldn't see.

He extended his arms, feeling for—

"Daddy!"

"I'm coming, Heather!" His hands found the doorframe, and from there, the light switch. The sudden brilliance hurt his eyes but he recognized his surroundings. Their house in Jacksonville. Before they'd moved to New York.

How did I—?

"Help!"

It didn't matter. With his bearings in place, he charged down the hallway, rifle in his hands. A thunderous roar shook the house.

He flung open her door and found her crouched at the top of the bed, eyes wide, as a giant beast emerged from her closet. Red eyes glowed like two hot coals and the hellish light illuminated the deadly curved talons and oversized fangs of the creature. The deathly smell of the thing stung his eyes.

Cuco!

No! Not here!

It wasn't possible, but somehow there it was. He had to save her before it stole her away. He ran to the bed and—

—Heather was gone. In her place crouched the boy, cowering among the tattered blankets and broken boxes. His tiny hands cradled the round, deadly object. Rob shouted at himself to stop but his body didn't listen. His finger tightened on the trigger, loosing a burst of rounds into the boy, whose body jerked as the fragmenting bullets carved through flesh and organs.

The boy opened his mouth and a single whispered word escaped.

"Bala."

His last breath gurgled out in a gush of blood. His head fell back and his hands opened. The grenade turned into a rubber ball.

Rob reached for it and then gasped when he saw his hands had morphed into monstrous paws with razor sharp claws that gleamed in the moonlight.

Beyond them, Heather's dead eyes stared at him through a mask of blood, her body torn to pieces.

No, this can't be happening. I'm not the devil.

I'm not El Cuco!

Not the-

"Rob! Wake up!"

Rob's eyes snapped open. Blinding light. For a dizzying moment Rob's dream world superimposed itself on reality. Then the nightmare shattered, leaving only the familiar sight of his kitchen and Allison kneeling next to him.

"Rob!"

"I'm okay," he gasped, although he wasn't. Not yet. Too much of the other place still remained, clinging to him like his sweat-soaked pajamas.

"Jesus, you scared the hell out of me. That must have been one helluva nightmare."

You're telling me. He squeezed her hand and then used the counter to steady himself as he stood. His body trembled from adrenaline overload. Colored spots whirled in his vision, pulsing in time to his racing heart.

Another sleepwalking episode. No denying it, they were getting more frequent. And worse.

He took a series of deep breaths, a trick his old psychiatrist had taught him at the VA hospital, when he'd first come home from Iraq. "*Let the fear flow out. With each breath, the anxiety departs and calm fills you.*"

Two more exhalations and the tightness in his chest eased. The pounding in his temples faded.

"I'm sorry," he said, when he could finally speak.

"It's okay." Allison kissed him and squeezed his hand. She started to say something else, when a terrified cry came from down the hall.

"Oni! Oni!"

Allison groaned. "Right on schedule."

She left to check on Ken. He suffered from nightmares as well, had since the day they brought him home. Unlike Rob, he never remembered them when he woke. Dr. Ellinger believed that was related to his partial amnesia, the blank spot in his memories of the night his family was murdered.

Rob took another breath and then jumped when his police radio blared.

"All units! Possible 10-27 at thirty-one Mason Street. All units respond."

Two seconds later, his work cell went off as well, signaling an urgent call.

A cold ball of fear formed in Rob's stomach. As if his dream had been a premonition, he knew what he'd hear even before he answered. 10-27. Code for violent crime.

There's been another murder.

The unwelcome image of clawed hands and red eyes appeared in his head.

There's no such thing as monsters.

Twenty minutes later, as he clenched his teeth to keep from puking, he wished he could believe those words.

"Is it really possible for childhood terrors to follow you into adulthood?"

Even as he asked the question, Rob's brain supplied the obvious answer.

Of course it is, cabron. *That's why you're here.*

Dr. Ellinger's half-smile told him the same thing, in a less condescending manner.

"Okay, stupid question." Rob settled himself deeper in the overstuffed recliner. Across from him, the psychiatrist occupied a matching chair, although he never extended the footrest.

"Not at all." Ellinger leaned forward, his movements half-hidden in the murky light of the office's single lamp. Heavy curtains covered the wide windows, and Rob wondered if they'd ever been opened. The whole office held the musty smell of a vacation home that had been closed up all winter. And something else, a vague, off-putting odor like someone had forgotten to take out the garbage for a couple of days.

Rob forced his mind to stop wandering and focused on the doctor's words. It was his third visit since he started seeing Ken's doctor, and so far he'd experienced no relief from the nightmares or sleepwalking episodes that had plagued him on and off for weeks.

"The mind is a very complex thing. If it wasn't, my profession wouldn't exist." Ellinger peered over his glasses, saw his joke had fallen flat, and continued. "What we experience growing up plays a major role in shaping us as adults."

"I've done some terrible things as an adult. Does that mean something in my childhood set me on that path?" Rob didn't look at the psychiatrist. He found it easier to talk while staring at his hands, which were clenched in his lap.

"That's not what I was referring to, although anything is possible. But all the facets of your life—the way you were raised, your friends, your school years—are the building blocks of who you become. They made it possible for you to join the Army, do things others couldn't, keep yourself and your soldiers alive. To come home and start a family, become a police officer. They also shape who you are on the inside, the person who feels guilty and stressed now about some of those same things. You're not a bad man, Rob. Just a normal person who got thrust into some bad situations."

Easy for you to say. I'm the one who's losing his shit. Rob kept the thought to himself. No reason to be snarky.

Ellinger shifted in his chair and crossed his legs. The gleaming white of brand-new sneakers contrasted sharply with his faded Dockers. His movements sent faint traces of onions and cabbage and sweat wafting by, the lingering ghosts of a thousand lunches, years of sweat and breath. Rob bit back a smile as he remembered Ken's description of the odor, after the boy's first session with Ellinger for his own night terrors.

"He's okay, but his office smells like farts."

Probably a lot of them in that old chair, Rob thought.

"Your time in the Army and your childhood are

linked in a way." Ellinger continued. Something in his voice made Rob look up. He found the doctor staring intently at him.

"How's that?"

One bushy eyebrow rose. "Surely you've put the pieces together. You're a smart man."

Rob had, but he didn't like the answer. The idea of his grade school self still having such power in the present day upset him. It didn't seem right. Children were supposed to outgrow their fears, not carry them into adulthood like invisible parasites.

"I get how adults can sometimes have nightmares of things that scared them as kids. And that the things I saw, the things I did, in the war could also cause bad dreams. But I was over them. Everything was great. Why did they come back?"

Ellinger jotted something in his tiny notebook.

"Most childhood fears stem from feelings of being powerless. Kids live in a world ruled by giants who hold their lives in their hands. They need adults for everything—food, safety, shelter. In many ways, being in the military isn't so different. And now you feel helpless again. You haven't stopped the murders, so your brain dredges up the old feelings of inadequacy, the old fears. Only with guilt tossed in for good measure, because of Iraq. Your subconscious creates a representation of all that."

Rob sighed. "I see myself as the monster."

"Exactly." Ellinger pointed his pen at Rob. "In your dreams, you become the thing you've always feared the most, because it's the only way you can have the power. And the child not only represents the boy with the grenade, but also the children in town who have died. And, it's also—"

"Me." It made sense, in a twisted way, but understanding it didn't make Rob feel any better. Something inside him would rather be a deadly monster than face his fears? *Great. Sounds like I'm going cuckoo for Coco Puffs. Or Cocu Puffs, in my case.*

"What about Ken? That doesn't explain his dreams."

Ellinger shrugged. "His parents were murdered. His grandparents died a year later in a car accident. And he spent the next four years in an orphanage. That's enough to give anyone nightmares, especially a young boy. And dealing with his dreams may have helped trigger yours. Given your subconscious the idea, so to speak."

"So what do we do?" That was the big question, the one Rob needed answered. He had to get his life back in some semblance of order, for his family's sake.

"We need to get to the root of your fears, expose it, and convince your subconscious that these stressors pose you no threat. That will take time, because the subconscious is notoriously stubborn. In the meantime, I'll prescribe something to help you sleep."

Rob nodded, taking care not to show his dismay. Getting to the root of his fears? If he had to tell the doctor the truth, he'd never be cured.

Because no one would ever convince him that what he saw in that window on his eighth birthday wasn't real.

"How'd it go?"

Rob shrugged. He didn't like talking about his visits with the shrink. Allison deserved an answer, though. She and Heather suffered through his nightmares—and Ken's—as much as he did.

For the Navarro household, the wee hours of the morning had become something of a bad dream for everyone.

"He said some things that made sense. How my subconscious takes my anxiety from the military and now these crimes and twists it all around in my dreams as a way of release."

"So you're gonna keep seeing him?" Ken had started his sessions with Dr. Ellinger not long after they adopted him, when his nightmares manifested. He'd been on a list of therapists the school provided. When Rob's own nightmares started, it seemed easier to use his son's doctor than find another. And piggybacking their appointments made scheduling easier.

"I guess."

"Good. Hey, maybe we should all go. We can get a family discount."

Let's hope we don't need it.

An hour later, Rob was wondering if maybe family counseling wouldn't be such a bad idea.

"Dad! Mom!" Heather's outraged cry echoed down the stairs just as he and Allison sat down to watch the news after dinner.

"Uh, oh. Tropical Storm Heather is moving this way." He rolled his eyes as her footsteps pounded down the stairs.

"Did you know about this?" Heather, her blue eyes aflame, held Ken's cell phone out. He was three steps behind her, his normally sunny expression replaced by an uncharacteristic pout and eyes that threatened tears.

"About what?"

"Ken and his loser friends crashing Chrissy's party. Tell me it's some kind of joke?"

"It's not a joke. Carol told me that since Chrissy was having friends over, Eddie could do the same."

"See? I told you. I was invited." Ken crossed his arms and glared at Heather.

"Great. Way to ruin everything, jerk." She shoved his phone at him.

Ken's lips tightened and the tendons in his neck bulged. Without saying a word, he turned and left the room.

"Ken, wait." Rob stood up.

For the first time since they'd adopted him, Ken didn't listen. He just kept walking, his thin body military straight. From the back, in sweatpants and a t-shirt, his small size made him look much younger than fourteen.

"Heather, that was uncalled for," Rob said. "You better get your butt in there and apologize to him."

"Apologize? But Dad, this party was supposed to be—"

"You can say you're sorry, or you can stay home." Rob made sure to use his special voice, the one that meant he'd reached his limit.

Heather looked ready to argue, but she recognized the imminent danger of being grounded. Instead, she stomped down the hall after her brother.

When she was out of earshot, Rob turned to Allison and let out a breath. "For a minute, I was afraid she'd call my bluff."

"You and me both." Allison giggled. "Good thing she doesn't know how much we're looking forward to having the house to ourselves."

"You can say that again." Rob fell into his recliner and hit the remote.

"Police still have no leads regarding the three missing children. Chief—"

He quickly switched the channel, scrolling down until he came to a movie station playing *Beer Fest*.

Mindless slapstick. The perfect antidote to all the darkness in his life lately.

Yet despite the hilarious antics onscreen, he couldn't shake the image of a faceless dead child from his thoughts.

CHAPTER FOUR

AT TEN MINUTES to midnight, Heather Navarro could hardly control the shivers running through her body.

The party had gone exactly as Chrissy planned. All the boys showed up and one of them brought a couple of scary DVDs to watch. There'd been no time for any real fooling around, not with Chrissy's parents constantly checking on them, but Steph Jones had made it clear he was interested in her, and he and his friends would be back later to continue the party, after Chrissy's parents went to bed.

That alone made the whole night worthwhile. The fact that Eddie, Ken, and the third member of their loser trio, Jaime Black, stayed upstairs in Eddie's room was an added bonus. She'd pretty much forgotten they were even there.

By the time Fred George sent the boys home at

just after ten-thirty, Heather felt sure it would end up being one of the best nights of her life.

The wait until midnight had dragged on for like a thousand years. Acting like everything was normal, pretending to sleep, trying unsuccessfully to keep from giggling. Listening to the house go silent around them. Watching the patio door as midnight approached.

Another nervous tingle raced down Heather's back. She'd already decided that if Steph wanted to, she'd let him into her pants. No further, though. She wondered if he'd want a blowjob. She'd never done that, although Chrissy had showed her how, using her fingers to demonstrate. She said she'd done it with Todd Devins a couple of times over the summer. And she'd probably do it again tonight.

Out of the other four girls—Cassie Johnson, Sherry Roper, Jada Williams, and Ellie Parsons—only Ellie had gone past getting felt up. She'd let a senior finger-bang her at a party the previous month. Except she'd been kind of wasted when she did it, and couldn't remember if it felt good or not.

Will it feel good with Steph? Heather wondered, checking the clock again. What if it hurt or—

Tap-tap-tap

Sherry let out a startled *yip* and immediately covered her mouth with her hands.

"They're here!" Chrissy whispered. She hurried to the sliding glass door, where five indistinct figures waited. Like the other girls, Heather had changed into strategically tight sweat pants and a tiny sleeveless t-shirt. Even in the dim light from the single bulb burning in the hallway, the boys would be able to see that none of them wore bras.

The butterflies in Heather's stomach raced around even faster as Chrissy opened the door.

"All right, let's get this party started!" Todd held up a large bottle of cola. "We swiped some rum from my dad's liquor cabinet."

The boys filed in behind Todd and took seats on the floor. Despite how the night had cooled considerably, Chrissy left the door open. In the event her parents came down to check on them, the boys would be able to exit fast.

Heather found herself torn between hoping they didn't get interrupted, and hoping they did. The way she was feeling, watching Steph as he parked himself across from her, she wasn't sure she'd have enough willpower to say no if he decided he wanted to go further than she'd planned.

Captured by Steph's eyes and smile, she didn't notice the bottle going around until someone placed it in her hand. She sipped without thinking and then choked as the bitter-sweet drink burned her throat.

"Shhhh!" hissed Chrissy, grabbing the bottle from her. "You'll wake my parents up!"

Mortified that she'd be the cause of the party getting ruined, Heather grabbed a pillow and shoved it against her face to muffle her coughs. Everyone remained silent, waiting for the sound of footsteps upstairs. When a couple of minutes passed and nothing happened, the whispered conversations started again.

Someone touched Heather's thigh, and she turned to see Steph sitting next to her. When had he moved?

"You okay?"

She nodded, unable to form words. He smiled. "Cool. 'Cause you'll need your mouth when we play this."

He held up a glass soda bottle. A few *ooohs* and *aaahs* greeted the sight of it. Heather's butterflies moved lower.

Spin the bottle.

"I'll go first," Steph said, while everyone else formed a circle. Somehow, the boys managed to make it boy-girl-boy-girl all the way around without saying a word.

They had this planned.

Steph gave the bottle a spin and everyone watched it go around until it stopped with the narrow end pointing toward Pete. There were a few giggles and someone asked if the two of them wanted to be alone.

"Spin again, dude." Todd took a sip of the rum and cola mix.

Steph gave the bottle a hard spin, and Heather's guts tightened. *Me-me-me—*

It stopped, pointing right at her.

Someone whistled and whispers of "*Kiss! Kiss!*

Kiss!" filled their circle, sounding deafening in Heather's ears. Before she knew what was happening, Steph's lips pressed against hers and something warm and wet pushed into her mouth. She responded to the kiss without thinking, her tongue meeting his in a rapid, playful dance. She closed her eyes and leaned forward, the material of their shirts no barrier to her breasts pressing against his chest. One of his hands went around her waist and pulled her closer.

Blinding light filled the room.

"I knew you had boys down here!"

Heather jumped away from Steph, her heart leaping into her throat. *Caught! Now her parents would find out and—*

"What the hell are you doing, you little troll?"

Heather's vision returned in time with Chrissy's words. Three people stood at the entrance to the family room. Thankfully, none of them were Chrissy's parents.

One of them, however, was Ken.

"You snuck boys in." Eddie George pointed at them. "Dad's gonna ground you for life."

"You would tell, wouldn't you?" Chrissy stood up, and Peter Harwood said something about them getting the hell out of there before they got caught.

"Wait." Everyone turned toward Steph. "I've got an idea. Let them hang with us for an hour. They can play a game with us."

"What?" Chrissy glared at Steph, her hands

planted on her hips. "Why the hell would I want my snot-nose brother and his friends around?"

Steph looked at Eddie. "'Cause if we let them play for a while, they won't tell your parents we were here, right?"

Eddie nodded, a suspicious smile on his face like he couldn't believe Steph was telling the truth.

"All right, dudes, take a seat. We were just trying to decide what game to play. My vote is for hide and seek."

"Hide and seek?" Heather leaned over and spoke in Steph's ear. "Why would we play that?"

"'Cause you and I can hide in a closet someplace," he whispered back. Pointing at the three new comers, he said, "We'll hide, and you three try to find us."

"What's hide and seek?" Ken asked.

"You never played hide and seek?" Body's voice echoed the surprise showing on everyone's faces.

"He's from Japan," Heather reminded him. Pretty much everyone in their school knew their family had adopted Ken earlier in the year. But sometimes they forgot, because he spoke perfect English, thanks to having an American mother and then living first with American grandparents and then in the foster home.

"That's right!" Steph leaned forward. "Can you play the Japanese version? Hitachi something. The one with the teddy bear and the devil."

Ken frowned. "Hitori Kakurenbo?"

"Yeah, that's it! I saw a story about it on the History Channel."

"I know the rules," Ken said. Something in his tone caught Heather's attention. He sounded...off. Why would a child's game bother him? Then Steph grabbed her hand and stole all her attention.

"All right. This is gonna be great!"

Despite an intense desire to escape into oblivion until morning, Rob held off on taking his pill until Allison announced she was calling it a night. The instructions said to only use it when you wanted eight hours of uninterrupted sleep, and he feared taking it too soon might lead to unwanted side effects. Like passing out during sex.

So it wasn't until eleven-thirty that he popped the little yellow tablet, brushed his teeth, and crawled into bed next to a content but sleepy wife.

Halfway through *Saturday Night Live*, Rob felt his eyelids grow heavy. An intense lassitude came over him, a feeling similar to when he took Nyquil for a cold. Allison had already been snoring softly since the last commercial break.

Okay, drugs, do your stuff.

He turned off the TV, rolled over, and settled into his pillow.

His last thought was a wish for dreamless sleep.

CHAPTER FIVE

"HITORI KAKURENBO?" The moment the words passed his lips, a dark, creepy feeling woke up in Ken's stomach. It grew worse when he told the boy with the spiky blond haircut that he knew the rules. A sense of foreboding came over him, a word he knew from books but that he'd never applied in his real life. Yet he recognized it immediately.

Something bad is going to happen.

Then the rational part of his mind spoke up.

You're just being silly.

He knew the cause of his anxiety. Although he remembered very little from the night his family was killed, he knew he'd been playing Hitori Kakurenbo at the time. His brother Toshio had taught him the game, and he'd wanted to play so he could brag to his friends about it in school on Monday. He'd been hiding in the closet when the burglar broke in, the one who'd been surprised by his parents and Toshio, and then stabbed them to death.

The police who found him, and the doctors who talked to him later, all told Ken the same thing: *"You are a lucky boy, Kenji. If you hadn't been hiding in the closet, you'd be dead, too."*

In a way, Hikori Kakurenbo saved his life.

So why did thinking about the game make him feel so frightened?

Because you associate it with the death of your family.

He didn't need Dr. Ellinger to tell him that. It was obvious. But knowing something and feeling something were two completely different things. Maybe it was because there was still so much of that night he couldn't remember. Things the doctors said he'd blocked out because they were too awful for his mind to hold on to. He used to think the memories would eventually return. They hadn't, and over the years he'd grown used to those blank spots.

"What do we need?" the blond-haired boy asked.

"Um, a stuffed animal. Rice. Red thread and a needle." Ken paused as he tried to think of all the things they'd require. "Maybe I should write these down."

The blond boy looked at Eddie's sister, Chrissy.

"Get the kid some paper."

"There are two parts to Hitori Kakurenbo." Ken sat in front of a low coffee table that held all the items for the game. Jaime Black sat to his left and Eddie to his right. Heather and her friends knelt or sat in a half circle in front of them. Ken tried his best not to get distracted by the way the blond boy—*his name is Steph*, he reminded himself—had his arm around Heather. Seeing them like that bothered Ken. Not because he didn't want his sister to have a boyfriend. Something about the boy reminded Ken of certain kids he'd known in the orphanage, the ones who'd be nice during the day when everyone was around, and then pinch you or play tricks on you at night when they couldn't get caught.

"First you take the bear into the bathroom and place it in a tub or sink that has water in it. Then you say, 'Teddy, for the first game, I am it.' You say this three times." Ken held up the fluffy white bear Chrissy had gotten them, which he'd prepared by cutting it open and filling it with rice and some fingernail clippings, and then tying it up with red string. "The person who is it drops the bear in the water and then runs around the house shutting off all the lights."

"We can skip that," Steph said, and the older kids giggled or snorted laughter. Chrissy had already turned the lights off and shut the door at the bottom of the stairs.

"The person who is it counts to ten and then takes the knife," Ken pointed at the steak knife on the table, "and goes back into the bathroom."

"That's it?" a boy with long brown hair asked.

"No. You say "I found Teddy," and then you pull the bear out of the water and stab it. When you do that, you've won."

"Sounds pretty stupid to me," someone muttered, and everyone laughed again.

"Ignore him," Steph said. "Tell them the second part."

"Okay." Ken wondered again if playing Hitori Kakurenbo was a good idea. He'd tried telling them that only one person could play, that the house was supposed to be empty, but Steph said they all wanted to play, and besides, it was just a game, right? Ken explained how it could be dangerous with so many people when the *oni*, the demon, woke up, but that only made them all want to play even more, including Eddie and Jaime.

"A possessed teddy bear runs around the house? Coolest game ever!"

It *was* just a game. Demons weren't real. So why was he still scared?

"In the second half of the game, the bear is it and he has to find you. You must say "Now Teddy is oni" and then run and hide as fast as you can. Wherever you hide, you should have your glass of salt water or alcohol with you. And you have to stay hidden until sunrise or the oni will get you. No matter what you hear or smell, you cannot come out."

"Hear or smell what?" asked one of Chrissy's friends, a girl named Sherry.

"Footsteps," Steph said, before Ken could answer. "Growling. Burning matches. The bear becomes a demon, remember? It's running around the house looking for you. The show I watched said people hear all sorts of weird things. Some of them go nuts in their hiding places."

"I'll bet we hear a lot of strange noises tonight." A kid named Pete held up his hand and the boy next to him slapped it.

Confused as to why they'd be happy to hear an oni running through the house, Ken finished explaining the rules.

"If the oni comes for you, take a big mouthful of your drink and spit it on them, and then run to a new hiding place. In the morning, you return to the tub and spit all the water on the teddy bear and shout "I win!" Then you burn the toy."

"Burn it? Why?" asked Heather.

"Because it still has the demon in it."

"Well, what are we waiting for?" Steph held up his red plastic cup. All the older kids had filled cups from a bottle of soda, which they refused to share with Eddie, Ken, or Jaime, who had to settle for salt water.

"I'll be it," Steph said. He took the bear into the guest bathroom, where they'd filled the sink part way since there was no tub. After dropping the bear into the water, he returned, sat down on the couch, and counted to ten. In the near dark, it was almost impossible to tell his clothes from the cushions, making him look like a blond head floating in mid-air.

Ken's feeling of wrongness grew stronger, and only his desire not to embarrass Heather kept him from saying they should stop. After their argument the other night, he knew he had to be extra careful not to shame her in front of her friends.

Knife in hand, Steph returned to the bathroom. A minute later he came back. "Okay, I stabbed the bear. Now it's time to hide." He took Heather by the hand and led her out of the room, the other kids following in pairs.

"Where should we go?" Eddie asked.

"Your room," Ken said. "We'll hide in your closet. It's big enough for all three of us."

Eddie shook his head. "Chrissy said no going upstairs, we might wake my parents."

"We won't make any noise." All of a sudden, Ken wanted to be as far from the bathroom and the bear as possible. The air felt heavier and colder. A memory came and went, too fast and blurry for him to grasp. *Footsteps pounding down a hallway*. He grabbed his glass of salt water. "I'm going up there."

He hurried to the stairs, glad to see his two friends following him.

Once they were all jammed elbow to elbow in Eddie's closet, cups clasped in their hands, his anxiety eased a bit, enough for him to think he was silly for letting a game scare him.

Bad memories, that's all, he reminded himself. *There*

are no such things as demons.

Still, he wished he hadn't told them about the game. Or let Heather go off with Steph. What if she got hurt?

She can't, silly. What can hurt her?

Downstairs, something thumped.

Jaime's body twitched, jostling Ken's arm. He gripped his cup tighter so it wouldn't spill.

"What was that?" Jaime asked.

"Probably someone sneaking food in the kitchen," Eddie answered. "You know what? I think Chrissy and her friends are gonna fool around with those guys. That's why they wanted to play this. This was just an excuse to have a big make out party."

Ken thought about the way Steph and Heather had been holding hands. The idea of the arrogant blond boy putting his mouth on Heather's bothered him to the point where he no longer felt nervous about the game.

Couldn't she see Steph was a jerk? She must know their parents wouldn't like him, because she'd never brought him to the house the way she did her other friends. Yet she kept staring all goofy-eyed at him.

Is she in love with him? Never having been in love with a girl, Ken didn't know what it looked like. In the orphanage, a few of the kids had boyfriends or girlfriends, but they had to hide it because dating wasn't allowed. Of course, he'd seen plenty of people kissing—and more—in real life and in the movies.

A make out party.

He hoped Heather wasn't making out with Steph.

Another thump sounded from somewhere, and a new thought entered Ken's head, one that wouldn't go away no matter how much he told himself he was being stupid.

I hope Heather isn't in danger.

With Steph's tongue dancing across her own, and his hand squeezing her breasts in a way that sent delicious shudders through her body, Heather's thoughts should have been focused totally on the pleasure of the moment. Instead, to her increasing aggravation, she found herself growing less excited by the minute, all because of Ken's freaky story about demons.

Each time she heard something bump or someone move, images of that stupid teddy bear appeared in her head. Running from room to room with the steak knife clutched in its paw, its button eyes glowing red as it peeked into closets and under furniture for someone to stab.

Stop it!

Steph's fingers closed tight on her nipple, too tight, and the pain doused her passion a little more. A line of drool escaped their joined lips and tickled her chin. Heather tried to regain the thrill from a few moments earlier, before her lust started to fade.

Across the room, someone coughed and whispered "Oh, my god!" Another person laughed and said, "It wasn't me, babe."

"What happened?" Chrissy's voice.

"Someone farted. It smells like death in here."

More laughter followed. Something went thump in the den. The noise bothered Heather because she couldn't recognize it.

A person? Chrissy's parents?

A foul odor seeped into the closet. Steph pulled away and turned his head toward the door.

"Whoever that is, knock it off. You're stinkin' up the whole place." He returned his mouth to Heather's lips. She backed up, intending to tell him she wanted to stop, or at least go somewhere that didn't smell like roadkill, when a new sound reached them. It took her a moment to identify it, and when she did, it made no sense.

Static.

Someone had turned on the television.

Another thump. This one much louder. At the same time, the stench in the room intensified.

A feeling of dread enveloped Heather. *Something was out there!* She pressed herself tighter to Steph, out of fear rather than desire. He mistook her actions and slid a hand under the waistband of her sweats, down to the damp spot between her legs. A shiver ran through her that had nothing to do with his fingers and she squeezed her legs shut. Steph pressed harder, but she kept her legs together, fighting conflicting emotions. It was what she'd wanted, what she'd planned on doing, but not like this. Not in a stinking closet with someone outside the door who might hear them.

"Stop," she whispered into his neck. In response, he shifted his position so her thigh was between his legs and his hand was free to move with more urgency. At the same time, he started rubbing himself against her. She felt his hardness through his jeans.

"Stop." She said it louder. Using both hands, she pushed him away.

"What the hell's your problem?"

"Not now. Not in here. Let's go to the couch or something."

"No way. The brats are out there." He leaned forward and smashed his lips against hers, jamming his tongue into her mouth. With his full weight against her, she found herself pinned against the wall of the closet, grabbing onto coats and jackets to keep from falling. He forced her legs apart and slid his knee between them before she could close them again.

This time there was nothing gentle about the fingers that rubbed against the lips of her vagina. She let go of the coats to punch his shoulders but his weight toppled her backwards. Shoes and boots dug into her back and his teeth cut her lips.

Clothing fell over them, tangling her arms and making it impossible to move.

Steph squirmed and wriggled, and for a moment she thought he was trying to dry hump her. Then she realized he'd pulled down his pants. His erection pressed against her again, only this time it wasn't against her thigh.

And she knew things were about to get a whole lot worse.

"Eww, Jaime, was that you again?"

"He who smelt it dealt it."

Eddie's elbow poked Ken's shoulder as the larger boy waved his hand in front of his face. Ken was about to tell him to keep still when the odor hit him. Faint, but potent. And nothing like the farts Jaime had been releasing all night. More like the stink of old food ripening in the hot summer sun for days.

The moment he smelled it, a bomb exploded in Ken's mind and all the mental walls he'd erected over the years came crashing down, releasing the dark secrets of his past.

Red eyes peering at him in the dark. The stench of death filling the air. Thumping footsteps. His parents and Toshio wailing in pain. The prehistoric growling. Blood on the kitchen floor as the police carried him through the kitchen. Looking over the policeman's shoulder and seeing his mother's leg all by itself.

Oni!

It all came thundering back, the repressed memories that until now had only escaped in bits and pieces through his nightmares, the ones he never remembered in the morning but had followed him like a curse through the years, growing stronger and more frequent as he grew older. In that instant, Ken remembered the awful truth about what he'd done as a boy.

And now he'd made the same deadly mistake again.

He opened his mouth and screamed.

Heather twisted to one side and Steph muttered a curse as he tried to get between her legs again. She opened her mouth to shout for help and instead found herself choking on the foul air.

Upstairs, a terrible scream shattered the quiet.

"Oh, shit!" Chrissy's voice. "Everyone get out. That's gonna wake my parents for sure."

"Dammit." Steph rolled off her, struggling to pull up his pants. A shuffling, snuffling noise sounded just outside the door, accompanied by another wave of grossness. Steph stood up and Heather grabbed him, a single thought running through her head: *Don't go out there!*

"Steph, wait." She fought her way out of the fallen clothes and grabbed his arm. "Don't open the door."

"Let go." He pulled away. "We're gonna get

caught."

"Something's out there."

"Stop being an idiot. The only people out there are—"

More thumping, much louder. Without warning, the door swung open. Heather threw up her arms and cried out, expecting the flash of a knife.

Mrs. George stood there, a furious glare plastered on her face.

"What the hell is going on?"

CHAPTER SIX

HEATHER SLUMPED IN the back seat of her father's Explorer, her arms folded across her chest. A heavy silence filled the car and the air practically burned with the fury emanating from her parents. She and Ken had already endured a heated lecture from their mother and several angry looks from their father. The one time Ken tried to interrupt and explain what really happened, he'd been told in no uncertain terms to keep his mouth shut. Eyes wide, he'd sunk down in his seat. The scolding had stunned Heather as well. Since his adoption, Ken had never once been reprimanded. Of course, he hadn't really needed to be, either.

"Necking in the goddamn closet? Drinking? What the hell got into you, young lady? And with your brother right there? I am mortified, do you hear me? Mortified? I hope you enjoyed yourself, because it's going to be a long goddamned time before

you leave the house again."

She imagined her friends were receiving equal earfuls of parental venom, and that none of them would be shopping at the mall anytime soon.

Now Heather wanted to say something, but she was afraid that even a single word would ignite her mother's wrath all over again.

The real problem was, she didn't know what to say.

That she was sixteen and making out with a boy wasn't a big deal? Or maybe go for the sympathy route and say Steph had forced himself on her. He had, in a way. Only Ken's nightmare had stopped him from date raping her. For that, she should be thanking Ken. Except all she felt was totally pissed off at him. If he hadn't woken Chrissy's parents, no one would be in trouble.

But you'd have been raped.

Maybe. Steph might have stopped on his own. Or she could have kicked him in the nuts.

It hadn't helped that Ken kept going on about demons, even after Heather tried explaining he suffered from nightmares.

"Not a nightmare," he said, over and over. "It was the oni."

Heather's own fears of monsters with knives had evaporated the moment the closet door opened, revealing nothing more dangerous than Chrissy's mother. At that moment, Heather wasn't sure if she felt more humiliated at being caught with a boy or because she actually fell for Ken's line of crap.

Despite the fact that she knew she'd be grounded for weeks, Heather breathed a sigh of relief when the car pulled into the driveway. She planned on spending the rest of the weekend locked in her room, and was already dreading going back to school. Steph would probably tell everyone he had sex with her, and Chrissy would make sure the whole sophomore class knew that Heather Navarro's crazy brother ruined her party and got them all grounded.

Maybe I'll just stay in my room forever.

Eddie George slammed his laptop shut and threw himself on his bed.

It wasn't fair!

Just because Chrissy had to break the rules and got caught with boys in the house, why did his friends have to go home, too? They hadn't done anything wrong. In fact, if Ken hadn't freaked out, nobody would have known about Chrissy sneaking the boys—or the liquor—in.

Sure, he and Ken and Jaime had known the boys were there and didn't tell, but no one liked a snitch. His father always said so. *"You have to stand up for yourself. You can't go running to a teacher every time someone calls you a name."*

So how come he was in trouble now for not telling?

Not fair. Not fair at all.

At least he wasn't grounded for a month like Chrissy. No mall, no parties, they'd even taken her phone away. She'd hollered and stomped her feet and slammed her door, which caused her father to shout at her, "That's another week! Wanna keep going?"

She'd been silent after that.

If only Ken hadn't freaked out and started screaming about demons. His sister said it was a nightmare, but he'd been awake right before that. They'd been making fun of Jaime for farting and—

Eddie paused. There was that smell again. Just like in the closet. Only it couldn't be Jaime, he'd gone home.

And it was getting stronger.

Heavy footsteps thudded in the hallway. Like someone stomping their feet. Something banged on the wall, and he jumped despite already knowing what was going on.

Chrissy was still pissed and she planned on taking her anger out on him 'cause it was his friend who ruined her party.

Well, screw that.

"Go away," he yelled.

Another bang answered him, this time so hard the pictures on his wall shook.

"You kids get to bed right now or so help me you'll both be grounded the rest of the goddamned year!"

More banging. He couldn't believe Chrissy wasn't listening to their father.

"Leave me alone," Eddie shouted. "Dad, it's not me!"

The door crashed open, sending broken pieces of wood through the air and revealing a creature worse than anything from a nightmare. Eddie tried to scream, but the sight of the monster, with its glowing red eyes and gaping, fang-filled mouth, stole his voice away.

A memory flashed through his head. His father pulling the knife out of the teddy bear and throwing the bear in the garbage while yelling at Chrissy about sneaking behind his back.

He released the demon.

The giant beast leaped at him.

And the only thing Eddie knew was pain.

Rob watched Allison turn off the light and climb into bed. He'd mostly kept quiet since they'd picked Heather and Ken up, afraid that saying the wrong thing might turn her wrath on him. In all their years of marriage, he'd never seen her so angry, not even the time his Uncle Ramon got drunk and threw up in the middle of Christmas dinner.

Of course, she had a good reason to be upset. Getting woken from your first sound sleep in weeks to come get your children was bad enough. Then finding out there'd been booze, boys, and who knew what else going on at the party?

What Heather had done was totally wrong and irresponsible, and she'd be suffering the consequences of her actions for a long time. But Allison seemed to be forgetting that screwing up was something every teen did, just like they experimented with alcohol and drugs and they always had sex on their brains. All you could do was try to teach them how to make sensible decisions. Screaming at them usually had the opposite effect, thanks to the natural resistance to authority inherent in teenagers.

In his mind, Ken was the bigger worry. They shouldn't be punishing him; he'd done nothing wrong. You couldn't expect him to call in the middle of the night to rat on Heather.

More importantly, there was the fact that not only had he remembered one of his nightmares, he suddenly recalled all the details of the traumatic events the night his family got killed.

"You know, this is something of a breakthrough for Ken," Rob ventured, hoping his positive words would distract Allison from her simmering fury. "I think we should call Dr. Ellinger and make an extra appointment. Now that he remembers that night, he'll need help coming to grips with it."

A moment of silence followed, and then Heather let out a long sigh that told Rob she not only knew what he was trying to do, she also realized that carrying on with her anger any longer would be over-reacting.

"That's a good idea. All that talk about demons has me worried." She reached out in the dark and felt around for his hand, took it and squeezed it.

Rob squeezed back. "It's weird. Ken's situation is a lot like mine. He thinks he saw a demon, an oni, kill his family. For me, it was a nightmare brought on by my fears about the children disappearing in town. All my grandmother's stupid stories convinced me I saw *El Cuco*, a boogeyman. We're both victims of our imaginations."

"I hope you're right." She rolled over, draping her arm across his chest. As her breathing slowed—she could fall asleep faster than anyone Rob had ever known—he stared at the ceiling, the unspoken part of her sentence stuck in his brain.

What happened if Ken continued believing in demons?

Will he end up like me?

"Mommy, Daddy! Help!"

Ken! Rob jumped up, ran to the hall. The hardwood floor cold against his feet.

Wood? Not carpet? Who's house is—?

Another terrified cry carved the darkness.

Down the hall. A door. Closed. Locked. Rob slammed it with his shoulder. Again. Again. It opened with a crash. He stumbled, fell inside—

Movement. A shadow on the other side of the bed.

The beast!

Enormous, hairy. Eyes like fire.

Cuco!

Rob reached for his gun. Nothing there. Drew his combat knife instead.

The demon roared—jagged teeth, so large—

The boy. Something in his hands.

Grenade!

No. Not this time. He's not the enemy. Rob darted around the bed. Charged the monster, the knife raised.

Terrible smell, rotten eggs and raw meat. Rob's stomach clenched.

"Bala." A child's voice. Calling him a demon.

No, I'm not! I'm not a—

The creature roared and came at him, claws extended. Rob prepared to meet his death.

"Ken! Get out of here! Run!"

"Rob!"

Allison's voice. No! Not her, too. He had to save them, even if it meant his own death. He leaped forward, thrust the heavy blade with all his strength. Their bodies collided, the demon's chest surprising soft.

"ROB!"

El Cuco exploded in a burst of light.

Rob bounced back and fell to his knees, whirling colored lights and the outline of a bed where his mortal enemy had stood just moments before.

Another nightmare. There was no monster.

He looked around.

Allison gaped at him from the top of Ken's bed,

her arms wrapped around the boy, both of them with their legs curled up and their eyes wide and frightened. In the doorway, Heather's face mirrored her mother's terror.

"What's wrong with—?" His words died as he noticed what they were looking at.

The carving knife embedded at the base of the mattress.

Allison came into the kitchen an hour later, dark circles under her eyes standing out against her sallow skin. Rob was waiting, a cup of coffee untouched between his hands.

"Are they asleep?" he asked. She nodded, avoiding eye contact as she poured herself a coffee.

After the episode in Ken's room, he'd sat at the table while she did her best to calm the children down. He'd waited, and thought hard about everything that was going on. And come to a reluctant conclusion.

The pills didn't work, Ellinger's counseling didn't work. Nothing did. Not for him, not for Ken. He had to try something different, and he'd come up with a solution.

They'd get out of town.

Not permanently, but for a few days. Maybe a week. Go somewhere far from Rocky Point, somewhere they could all reset and forget everything going on. He'd catch shit for leaving in the middle of an investigation, but as long as Ellinger said it was medically advised, they couldn't say no. And it would be good for Heather and Ken, too. Get them away from the darkness sitting over them, the whole town.

"Good. We need to talk." Before he could say the rest, she interrupted.

"Yes, we do." She looked up from her coffee. Her eyes were brimming with tears and yet hard and cold at the same time. When she spoke, her voice trembled.

"You need to leave."

CHAPTER SEVEN

"YOU NEED TO LEAVE."

Rob was still processing Allison's devastating ultimatum when his police radio went off, causing both of them to jump.

"All units! Possible 10-27 at Twenty-Two Dogwood. Reports of a loud disturbance and shots fired."

Allison gasped and Rob's body went numb. Twenty-Two Dogwood? That was—

"That's Carol and Fred's house," Allison said, her face going even paler. "You don't think—?"

The distant wail of police sirens shattered the early morning quiet. Before he could answer her, his phone buzzed.

"Navarro?" The moment he heard Chief Sloan's voice he knew the news had to be bad. Very bad. The chief wouldn't call at four in the morning except in dire circumstances. *"We've got another one.*

Get over there right now."

Rob's body went numb and he clutched the phone to keep from dropping it. *The Georges? Oh, my god. What—*

"—you there? Detective?"

"I'm... I'm here. On my way."

He lowered his hand and found Ken and Heather staring at him from the hallway. He tried to think of something to say, find the words he needed for his family.

Instead, all he could do was gather them in his arms and bite his lip as the tears ran down his cheeks.

The mournful dirge of the sirens only a few blocks away told them what he couldn't.

Rob sat on the lumpy, cheap motel mattress and watched as the television played the same grotesque scene that had been looping endlessly through his head all day.

Flashing red and blue lights painted the front of the Georges' house. A line of EMTs wheeled gurneys out the door to waiting ambulances. The bloody sheets covering the bodies informed viewers of the awful truth. Police officers stood helplessly on the front yard, while neighbors in bathrobes and sweats gathered behind yellow tape, stunned that Death had come to their quiet street.

Rob felt a moment of weird disconnect as he saw

himself exit the house, his face bone gray and hollow-eyed in the glare of the camera lights. If he hadn't been walking, he could have passed for one of the corpses.

"...police responding to calls of a disturbance at the home of Barbara and Fred George just after two a.m. discovered a grisly scene. All four members of the family murdered in gruesome fashion—"

Rob grabbed the remote and turned the television off.

"It's only temporary."

Allison's words reverberated in his head. The temptation to call home was a living thing inside him, and it took all his resolve to keep his hand off the phone. Conflicting emotions formed an acid pit in his stomach, burning worse than the Chinese takeout he'd picked up on the way to the hotel after his totally shit day ended in even shittier fashion when he stopped at home, thinking they could talk things out, only to find Allison standing firm on her decision.

"You need help. You can't be around us, not like this. Not until you're better. Please don't make things harder," she'd added, when he'd tried to object.

But he had.

There'd been shouting on both their parts. He'd been hurt, bone deep, soul deep by her charge that he was a danger to Ken and Heather.

"You tried to attack us with a goddamned knife!"

He couldn't deny that, but still his anger raged,

fueled by guilt, by a sense of betrayal, and most of all by the crushing loss of an entire family, people he knew, called friends, because of his own impotence. Staring at their ravaged, bloody corpses and then dealing with the case all day had left him drained of any positive emotions. To come home and suffer the indignity of being kicked out of his own house, to not even be able to comfort his children when they needed him...

That's when he'd reached his bursting point and accused Allison of using the sleepwalking as an excuse to finally get rid of him, that if she truly loved him she'd stand by him during the bad times.

At which point she'd started crying.

"No. God, no. That's not it." She'd grabbed his hands, gripped them tight. "I love you with all my heart. I want us to be a family forever. But the safety of the children has to come first."

Combined with her words, her tears doused the bitter flames burning inside him. Even now, when they threatened to rise up again, all he had to do was remember the knife, and how close he'd come to hurting someone, and they disappeared in a wave of cold reality.

She was abso-fucking-lutely right. He couldn't be trusted. Not now.

So he'd agreed to go. Promised to do whatever it took to get better, even if it meant seeing Ellinger every day or checking into a hospital for more intense treatment.

They'd done their best to explain things to Ken and Heather. Daddy was going to spend a few nights at a hotel so everyone could finally get some sleep without him waking them up. It was only until the doctors got his medicine right and he stopped having nightmares. But he saw the fear in their eyes. They'd heard the arguing, the accusations.

Watching their emotions play across their faces, he vowed to get better as fast as humanly possible so he could rebuild his family. He told Allison as much as she walked him to the front door.

Her last words to him were, "Do it faster than that."

Then she kissed him and shut the door, leaving him alone with his suitcase.

Rob leaned back against the fake wicker headboard, which creaked in protest. Two more hours until the kids' bedtime. He'd promised Allison he'd only call a couple of times a day. Enough to let them know daddy loved them, but not so much it became a burden. He wanted to use his last call for today to say goodnight.

He glanced at the bottle of sleeping pills. Should he take one now? Or wait? What if he took it and fell asleep too soon? Then he'd look like a jerk for not calling.

A guilt-mouse ran circles in his stomach. He'd started thinking of all his unwanted emotions—guilt, fear, anger, helplessness, despair—as rodents living inside his body, gnawing and scratching and building bigger and bigger nests. At first they'd all been mice; lately, there'd been more than a few rats in the mix.

"Fuck!" He threw an empty food container across the room. It struck the wall with an unsatisfying plonk. Garlic sauce sprayed out, the brownish-yellow splatter blending seamlessly with the peeling, stained wallpaper.

No pill. Not yet. He picked up the remote again and flipped through the channels, half of which were in Korean or Spanish, before settling on an old *Seinfeld* rerun.

Two hours. Then I call home and take the pill.

Allison stood at the foot of Ken's bed, watching him toss and moan his way through a sedative-induced slumber. Every plaintive sound broke her heart and rekindled her anger at her husband because he wasn't there to comfort them, comfort her, when she needed him.

Goddamn you, Rob. Why now? Why couldn't you have been stronger?

Then she instantly felt guilty for thinking such things. For being such a bitch. He'd been through more than she could imagine. First in Iraq and now seeing all those poor children torn to pieces. Was it a surprise he was falling apart? God knew she'd have gone off the deep end after seeing one body.

Maybe he should retire. Take the early package and find

another job.

"Oni. Oni." Ken mumbled the words then fell silent again. Just their luck, Ken finally remembered the traumatic events of his past and instead of curing his nightmares, it made them worse.

She'd called the psychiatrist, Ellinger, earlier. He'd said one of three things would happen. Ken would lose the memories again, he'd gain control of them, or he'd succumb to them and suffer from long-term delusions that might require hospitalization. It all depended on the strength of his makeup and how he responded to therapy.

"C'mon, Ken," she whispered. "Fight it. You're stronger than this."

As she spoke, it wasn't lost on her that they were the same words she'd been silently saying for her husband.

Inside Ken's dream-mind, a battle waged. Part of him, the little boy still frozen with fear in the closet while the demon killed his family, wanted to just hide forever. Sit quiet and safe in the dark until all the bad noises stopped and the sun chased the monster away. It worked before, it would work again.

The other part of him knew that if he kept hiding, more people would die. The oni wouldn't stop until everyone who'd been in the Georges' house that night was dead. And then it would go back to preying on the children in town.

Teenage Ken kept trying to force open the closet door but so far young Kenji was too strong. He'd had years of practice hiding from the truth, had built barriers even the oni couldn't get through.

Ken kept trying, though. He used everything he could think of. Giant hammers. Battering rams. His fists and feet. When that didn't work, he even tried punching his own younger self, only to see his hands pass harmlessly through little Kenji as if he were nothing but a hologram.

Beyond the blackness of the closet, on the other side of the door, people screamed and terrifying growls shook the floor. The horrible stench of the oni poisoned the air as the beast stomped back and forth through the rooms of their old house in Japan. Every once in a while, a red light filled the closet, coming from two giant eyes peering through the slats. On those occasions, Kenji slid further back and the force holding the door closed grew even stronger.

With a sigh, Ken sat down. As long as Kenji thought the monster was waiting for him, he'd never open the door. And if that happened, everyone they cared about—Mom, Dad, Heather, their friends—would eventually die horrible deaths at the claws of a monster no one even believed existed except him. And by the time they did, it would be too late.

There has to be a way to fix this.

He wished he could bring his real parents back.

They'd been so good at comforting him as a boy, just holding him and telling him everything would be all right...

Then it came to him. He'd been going about things the wrong way. All he'd been doing was scaring a frightened little boy even more.

He got up and went to where Kenji cowered on the floor. Wrapped his arms around his younger self and hugged him tight.

"Hush now, little one," he whispered, using Japanese for the first time in more than a year. "Hush now."

The same words his mother used to say when Kenji was sobbing from a bump or cut. A lullaby returned to him, one he'd always enjoyed when his mother sang it.

"Nennen korori yo, Okorori yo. Bōya way oi ko da, Nenne shina." Hushabye, hushabye. My good baby, sleep.

He sang it again, and again, feeling Kenji beginning to relax in his arms. By the fourth repetition, Kenji's eyes had closed. His body began to lose substance, becoming light as air and soft as a summer breeze. Ken pulled him closer, his past self becoming part of him again.

On the other side of the door, yellow light seeped in through the slats. The door slowly swung open, filling the closet with bright sunshine.

When Ken looked down, he was alone.

Ken opened his eyes and blinked. Outside, the sun was just rising over the rooftops. He sat up. The terror of knowing the oni was still on the loose remained inside him, along with his shame for bringing it into the world once again. Both threatened to overwhelm him, to send him back to the land of dreams where nothing could touch him. But now he had control, not six-year-old Kenji. The time of hiding was over.

He had to find a way to stop the oni and send it away for good.

But how?

CHAPTER EIGHT

HEATHER GASPED and jumped at the sound of tapping on her bedroom door.

It's him! He's coming for me!

"Heather? Can I come in?"

The invisible hands of fear relaxed their grip on her heart, allowing her to move and breathe again.

You idiot. Psycho nut jobs don't break in during the day. Or knock on the door.

"Sure, Mom." She set her brush down and turned as the door opened, revealing her mother standing there. Dark circles stained the flesh under her eyes and her brown hair was mussed. Smudged makeup gave evidence of recent tears wiped away.

"Here." Her mother held out Heather's phone. "Your father and I think you should have this back. Not because you deserve it, but so you can get in touch with us if you need to. This doesn't mean you're not still grounded."

"Thanks." Heather placed the phone on her dresser. Grounded or not, she had no intention of leaving the house after dark. Not until they caught the guy who'd killed her best friend.

Heather expected her mom to leave after that, but she sat down on the bed.

"Do you want to talk about it?"

"Not yet." Heather shook her head. She did want to talk, wanted to throw her arms around her mother and cry and tell her that she'd *almost died* for god's sake, but those feelings weren't ready to come out. They needed time to mature. Then they'd rise up and burst loose. If she let them out too soon, something would remain, festering inside her. Then she'd probably end up having nightmares for life, like Ken. Or her father.

When the time came, though...it'd be a doozy. She could tell that already.

"Okay." Her mother stood up and kissed her on top of the head. "Whenever you're ready, we're here, sweetheart." Then she was gone, leaving Heather alone with her thoughts and fears.

The temptation to run after her mother, just sit with her in a room so she wasn't by herself, came so suddenly she was half out of her chair before she realized it. Then she slowly sat down. Her mom had enough problems to deal with. Ken. Whatever was going on with her and dad.

Divorce? When Sherry's mother left, she never came back.

Is that gonna happen to us?

Heather took a deep breath. She could handle her problems for now. Besides, she had people she could talk to.

She grabbed the phone and hit the button next to Cassie Johnson's picture.

"Tell me more about El Cuco."

Just hearing the word made Rob twitch. Even more than thirty years later, he hated to say it. To think it. But he had no choice now. He took a deep breath, wondering how foolish he'd sound, then decided to just tell his tale. Surely a seasoned psychiatrist had heard crazier things. He wouldn't laugh.

At least not out loud.

"Growing up in Puerto Rico, parents told their children tales of El Cuco to make them behave. Go to sleep or El Cuco will come for you. Do your homework or El Cuco will eat you in the night. It's the monster under the bed, the boogeyman, and it steals little boys and girls. It also loves the taste of human flesh. There's even a lullaby about him: Sleep child, sleep now, or else El Cuco will come and eat you."

"That could certainly scare a small child."

"More like terrify," Rob said, remembering all the nights he lay awake in his bed after his *abuela*, his grandmother, closed the door, her gruesome lullaby still echoing in Rob's ears. Covers pulled up to his nose, listening for any sounds in the dark that might mean El Cuco had emerged from the closet or slid out from under the bed. In those days, sleep never came easy in the Navarro household.

And that was *before* he witnessed the beast in all its horrific glory.

"My grandmother was the worst. She'd describe El Cuco in detail, from its red eyes to its sharp nails and teeth. I think she loved scaring us, but by then my brothers were older and it didn't really work with them."

"It did with you, though, right?"

"Oh, hell yeah. I had nightmares all the time. It's a wonder I ever got any sleep."

"But the nightmares did come to an end. After your family moved to New York. Away from your grandmother. And the...events...happening in your town."

Events. That was one way of putting it. How many children had disappeared that summer? Fifteen? Twenty? Probably no one knew for sure. Things were different then. Especially when you lived in a poor country, and an even poorer village. Kids ran away. Crime was rampant. And the apathetic, under-trained police force had bigger problems, like gangs and drugs, to deal with.

"So, what? I'm gonna have nightmares and sleepwalking episodes every time someone in my town gets kidnapped or killed?" *Or I kill someone,* but they both left those words unsaid. "I'm a cop. Investigating murders is part of my job. I can't keep putting my family in danger just because my brain is fucked up."

"Your career choice isn't for me to say." Ellinger shrugged. "Just like I can't say when or if we'll put an end to the nightmares. All we can do is try."

"Great. And in the meanwhile? I'm on my last legs here. And I want to be with my family. They need me, and I need them." Rob rubbed his eyes, which he knew were bloodshot and baggy. He'd caught a glimpse of himself in the rearview mirror when he parked the car and he'd been shocked at how much he resembled a drunk. Or a *lunático*.

Not the best look for a cop dealing with a high-profile murder investigation.

"Well, let's work on that first. I'm going to give you a different sleep aid. I wouldn't prescribe this for long term use, but for a couple of weeks it won't hurt you. And if you don't have any episodes the first few nights, we can see about lowering the dosage."

"I hope to God they work." Rob read the name scribbled on the paper. *Somnia*. It sounded familiar. Probably from TV commercials. "The other ones sure as hell didn't."

"Well, these are much stronger."

"Any side effects I should know about?"

"Not typically. Just make sure you don't drink any alcohol with them, and don't take them if you're going to be driving. If you experience nausea or lightheadedness, let me know."

A small chime sounded before Rob could respond.

"That's our time for today." Ellinger stood and held out his hand. "I'll see you and Ken two days from now. Hopefully you'll both have good news."

"Yeah." Rob shook the doctor's soft, clammy hand and exited the office. While he waited for the elevator, he couldn't help thinking back to that night in Puerto Rico.

Surrounded in darkness. Feeling like the walls were moving closer, shrinking the room until nothing existed except his bed. Every sound magnified by his terror. It was hot in the room, too. He wanted to get up and open the window, but that meant putting his feet within reach of anything hiding under the bed.

But it was so hot, he'd never be able to sleep.

Mustering his courage, he stepped out of bed and lifted the window.

And looked right into a pair of eyes that burned bright red against the black night.

Cuco!

The breeze brought the smell of the beast to him, a nasty mix of unwashed bodies and rotten food, like the stinky dumpsters behind the restaurants in town.

A hairy arm reached up, giant claws extended—

Something touched Rob's arm and he let out a startled gasp. Bright light burned away his childhood bedroom and returned him to the present. The elevator doors were open and people were moving past him. A few cast puzzled looks in his direction.

Great. Now I'm the crazy guy leaving the shrink's office.

He stepped inside and purposely kept his back to everyone, although he could sense their judgmental gazes.

All the way home, he kept checking his mirror.

For red eyes.

"Can you believe it? Like, the guy was probably in the house the whole time and—"

Cassie Johnson paused in the middle of her sentence as she saw Heather approaching. The circle of girls she'd been holding court to all turned and looked.

"Heather! Ohmygod, you came to school. I thought I was the only one."

Heather nodded. By only one, Cassie meant the kids who'd been at Chrissy's party. All the other parents had kept them home, for reasons ranging from psychiatrist appointments to just taking some time to be together, which was parent-speak for a guilt-free way to extend the weekend another day. Heather and Ken had been given the choice to stay at home or go to school, and they'd both chosen school.

"Yeah, but can we talk about something else? Anything? I need a break from it all."

"Good luck." Cassie waved a hand at the bustling hallway. "It's totally viral. We're like, heroes or something. There were reporters at my house yesterday."

"Mine, too."

"Did you really hear the killer?" a girl asked. Heather recognized her from gym class but couldn't be sure of her name.

"I don't know." It was the same thing she'd said to the reporters, and her parents, and police. She'd told them she and Steph had been hiding in the closet ("Just kissing, I swear!") and they'd heard sounds in the other room. They thought it was Ken and Eddie and Jaime playing their stupid game. But then Ken screamed and the next thing they knew, Mrs. George opened the closet.

"I heard he tore them all to pieces," someone said.

"I heard he killed Eddie first, and then the parents, and he saved Chrissy for last."

"Caught her under the bed." "Dragged her body down the hall." "Ate pieces of them." "Did your dad really see the bodies?"

The words came from all directions, too fast for Heather to keep up with who said what.

"I gotta go." She pushed through the growing crowd to her locker. From there she went to the bathroom, where she sat in a stall and focused on not crying until the warning bell rang for first period.

The rest of the day went much the same. Everyone wanting to ask her about the murders or tell her their version of them. Classes passed like hazy dreams, with only half her attention on the lessons. She couldn't stop thinking about what had happened.

I was there. Right there, when... whoever... was prowling through the house. Those noises. The TV going on. All him!

I could have died.

Died.

That's what it all came down to. Only luck and a nightmare had saved her. Saved all of them. The police had no idea why the killer waited until they all left before attacking the Georges. The news reporters speculated he might have gotten spooked by the Georges waking up, that he'd planned on killing them one or two at a time while they were hiding.

I could have died.

By the time the final bell rang, she couldn't wait to get home and just be with her family. For the first time in her life, the idea of not being allowed out didn't seem so bad.

Not with a crazy murderer still on the loose.

Chapter Nine

SHERRY ROPER opened her eyes to a red glow illuminating the darkness of her room.

Eleven minutes after one.

The triple digit number on her clock stayed with her even after she closed her eyes again. 111. A weird time to wake up. A chill washed over her and she pulled the sheets up to her chin. She hated that her father always kept the air conditioning so jacked up it felt like winter inside. Why did she have to freeze her ass off just because he was hot at night? Maybe if he lost some weight he wouldn't sweat so much.

She couldn't open the window because that "wasted energy, dammit." And if she closed the ceiling vent it would get too warm.

And now she had to pee. Great.

She got out of bed and tip-toed to the bathroom.

Her father had to be up at five for work, so she was careful not to make any noise. She didn't even flush the toilet. Back in bed, she found sleep impossible. Thoughts of Chrissy kept circling, how they'd all been right there while a killer stalked them. The same psycho the police said was responsible for the kids who'd been chopped up or gone missing the past several months.

We got lucky. So lucky.

What if he's out there right now? She glanced at the window. *What if he's on my street?*

In my house?

Something creaked downstairs and her heart kicked. Another sound, this time behind the wall. *Tap. Tap. Tap.* Like a knife against wood, someone lurking in the hall, getting ready to—

No. It's just the pipes. Stop being an idiot.

Thump.

Definitely not the pipes that time. Was her father up? Sometimes he had to—

Squeeeeeak

Her bedroom door slowly opened. Someone stood there, a dark, faceless shadow filling the doorframe.

"Dad?" Had she woken him after all?

Twin circles of red appeared. A horrific odor assaulted her, the same terrible stench she'd smelled at Chrissy's house.

The shadow entered her room and revealed its true form.

And Sherry knew her luck had run out.

It leaped onto the bed, its roar drowning out her screams.

By the time Karl Roper reached his daughter's room, only pieces of her remained.

"Help!"

Rob ignored the girl's terrified cry. Moonlight turned his claws to silver as he raised his massive hands, prepared to—

The dream fell apart, the girl's face fading away, leaving him alone in the darkness.

Dark! But I left the television on when I went to sleep.

He struggled to get his bearings. Soft carpet under his feet. In the dream, there'd been sand. Then wood. Hot desert air and then the cool kiss of air conditioning painted with hints of candy-scented perfume, which still lingered in his nose.

That girl. Her room? Who—? He tried to remember her face. It danced just out of reach, his dream-memory already turning hazy, blotting out the details. She'd seemed familiar, as if he should know her...

The details around him grew clearer as his eyes adjusted to the dim light. A desk with a laptop and papers. Clothes hanging over the chair. A nightstand with books piled next to a lamp.

Not a stranger's room.

Ken's.

Soft breathing came from the bed, and he made

out Ken's face against his pillow, eyes closed, hair flat from his evening shower.

Realizing where he was brought another fear-rat to life in his stomach. If Allison discovered him in the house, there'd be no reasoning with her.

Divorce city.

Rob backed toward the door and then stopped as a wave of dizziness came over him. He reached out to grab the corner of the desk and for the first time noticed the object in his hand.

A knife!

The long, heavy blade hit the desk with a thump. The sound wasn't loud, but in the silence it reverberated like thunder in his ears. Ken's breathing changed and he opened his eyes.

"Dad? Did you see the oni?"

"Shhh," Rob whispered. "Go back to sleep."

"Okay." Ken's eyes closed and he rolled onto his side. Rob counted to ten. When nothing further happened, he crept out of the room, grateful for the nightlight Allison always left on in the hallway. Once he reached the stairs, he tiptoed down and made his way through the living room to the front door, which stood slightly open.

Outside, door securely locked behind him, the weight of his subconscious actions crashed down and he fell to his knees, his eyes squeezed shut as he fought control of his breathing.

Can't stay here. Can't let Allison find me like this.

That thought, more than anything, halted his

incipient panic attack before it could explode. He stood up and patted his pockets. Nothing. No keys, no wallet. He must have used the spare key in the fake rock next to the porch.

How would he get home? He wasn't even wearing shoes, just the previous day's pants and shirt. His motel was three miles away. If a cop saw him, they'd arrest him for vagrancy.

Suck it up and do it, his inner voice said. *You got here, didn't you? Worry about your feet later.*

But first, get rid of that knife.

He looked at it again, this time recognizing it as part of the set in their kitchen. The blade gleamed like chrome in the moonlight.

He went to the nearest sewer grate, the grass cold and damp against his feet. Dropped it down, the clink of metal on metal somehow the guiltiest sound he'd ever heard.

Then he headed for the corner, doing his best to stick to the shadows.

Only after he was back in his motel room, his blistered, burning feet soaking in a tub of cold water, did he break down and cry.

Rob sat naked on his bed and stared at the wall. Every light in the room was on, despite the dawn seeping in from around the curtains. An empty can of soda rested in his hand.

All to make sure he didn't fall asleep.

Another nightmare, another episode of sleepwalking, with no memory of what he'd done.

The knife. The little girl. Waking up in Ken's room.

No matter how hard he tried, everything between falling asleep in his room and waking by Ken's bed remained a blank.

How long was I sleepwalking? And what did I do?

Rob stared, but it wasn't the shitty motel room he saw, it was his memories. The slow but steady downhill road that had taken him to this place, this hell where he teetered at the edge of a cliff, inches away from losing everything he loved.

All his life he'd been shadowed by death. Ever since that night after his eighth birthday, when he'd woken to see that... creature peering in through his open window. The horrible face, the terrifying red eyes. He'd screamed, woken the whole family, his grandmother had come and calmed him. His brothers just laughed and called him a baby.

"Miedo a los monstrous!" they'd teased. Afraid of monsters.

He might have believed them, that he imagined everything, if a child hadn't been reported missing the next day.

No one made much to do about it, not even when the second child disappeared.

But when it happened a third time, people started talking. Serial killer. Child predator. *Lunático*.

But deep down, Rob knew the truth. A real monster was out there. And as the disappearances mounted, and the first bodies showed up torn apart, with pieces missing, the kids at school stopped joking and started whispering about El Cuco. Which only made Rob's nightmares worse, to the point where he slept with the light on all the time.

Finally, his grandmother showed him how to place a glass of salt water with an egg in it under his bed—a traditional protection against evil—and he kept one there every night, and another in his closet.

The talismans helped, at least to the point where he could get some sleep each night. Although more than once he woke up from a nightmare of blood and death, certain he smelled the rotten stench of the beast or caught a glimpse of a deformed shadow moving past his window.

For the Navarro family, El Cuco never returned.

Until now.

Except that wasn't true, either. El Cuco didn't exist. Nothing had come back except his own shit-poor coping skills. Monsters weren't real. It was all in his head. Stress-induced episodes.

What about the knife?

He didn't want to think about that. He hadn't hurt himself. Or the children. Or Allison.

Why did you have it?

"I don't remember!" The words came out in a shout and he clamped a hand over his mouth. Not good to wake the neighbors at five-thirty in the morning.

An image of the girl, her face fuzzy but familiar...

Maybe you should turn on the news.

"No." That was the last thing he wanted. Just more stories about how the police weren't doing their jobs, *he* wasn't doing his—

Click

His finger pressed the remote even as his brain said no. Fear and relief warred inside him as each story passed with no new unsolved murders or disappearances reported. Sports, politics, international news. He closed his eyes and let out a sigh. That was it. Soon the first of several morning talk shows would start over and he'd get in the shower, prepare for another day at work. Maybe they'd actually find—

"—repeating our top story, another vicious crime has rocked the quiet town of Rocky Point."

Rob's eyes snapped open.

"Sixteen-year-old Sherry Roper was brutally murdered in her bedroom while her father slept down the hall. Police say the father, Karl Roper, woke to the sound of his daughter's screaming and a man shouting.

"It sounded like a bear attacking her," Roper told police. "It couldn't have taken me more than a minute to get to her. But it was too late. My daughter..."

The camera cut to a shot of a residential street, one that Rob knew all too well. He'd been there plenty of times, dropping Heather off or picking her up at the blue house with the red shutters, the one now cordoned off by police tape.

Sherry Roper. She'd been one of the girls at the

party. His brain, still working in slow motion from the sleeping pill and being up all night, finally put a face to the name. Black hair in ringlets. Too many earrings for Rob's taste.

The girl from his dream.

Jesus Christ.

Did you do it?

I don't know.

But you think so.

No. I couldn't—

The knife falling into the sewer.

Has it been me all along?

Am I the boogeyman?

No! Stop thinking like that.

On the TV, the story continued.

"Chief Emery Sloan spoke briefly at the crime scene, saying there would be a press conference at three o'clock.

"In the meantime, we are doing everything possible to put an end to these heinous crimes. We are looking at several suspects and we hope to have more information by this afternoon."

Suspects? Rob frowned. That was news to him. As of the previous day, there'd been no new leads at all. What had turned up in the meantime? And why hadn't he been told?

For that matter, why hadn't he been called when

—

His phone buzzed with an incoming text message. His stomach lurched when he saw it was from Allison. There was only one reason for her to contact him. She knew he'd been at the house and —

> Rob. The police just left. They were looking for you. I had to tell them.

He had just enough time to get dressed before a heavy fist pounded on the hotel room door, making Rob jump.

"Detective Robert Navarro. FBI. Open the door. We need you to come with us."

Chapter Ten

THE FACES OF the three men sitting across the table held a mix of expressions.

Suspicion. Sympathy. Anger.

All the same emotions Rob would have felt if he'd been one of them, instead of the man being questioned.

The fact that he knew them, worked with them, only made his fear worse. For them to treat him like a suspect meant they were already half-convinced he did it.

Did you? Did you kill her?

Doing his best to ignore the increasingly strident voice in his head, he sipped his coffee and regarded the trio. Chief Emery Sloan, Detective Alan Woods —Rob's old partner from their patrol days—and Assistant Special Agent Edgar Choi, the local FBI office's liaison for the case. Rob had worked with him once before, on a dignitary protection assignment when the Vice President spoke at a town hall during the previous election campaign.

"Let's go over this again, Detective," Choi said, glancing down at his notes. An affectation, since he obviously had the whole story memorized by that point. They'd been grilling Rob for more than an hour, had heard his statement twice already.

"Three time's a charm?" Rob rubbed his eyes, which were gritty from lack of sleep.

"This isn't a joking matter, Navarro," Chief Sloan said with a scowl. He looked as wrung out as Rob felt, with bags under his eyes and sweat stains under his arms.

"Yeah, I know. Look, I'll say it again. I don't know how my car got there. I was at the hotel. Asleep."

He'd been stunned speechless when he'd been informed that his car had been found three houses down from the Roper murder scene. Keys in the ignition.

"So, what? Someone broke into your hotel room, took your keys and nothing else, and stole your car? And this person just happened to abandon it next to a murder scene?"

Rob shook his head. He understood their strategy, had used it plenty of times himself on suspects. Hammer them over and over with the same questions until they slipped up on one of the details. In the meantime, other officers would be checking out his alibis for the times of the other murders.

"Maybe I left the keys in the car. I've had a lot on my mind lately." Although no one had asked him yet, they obviously knew from Allison the reason he'd been sleeping at a hotel. Which meant they knew about his nightmares and possibly even his sleepwalking. Did they also know about the knife incident? How much had Allison told them?

"Were you high last night?" The question came from Woods.

"You know I don't do drugs. What the actual hell?" Rob looked at his old partner. They weren't what you'd call friends. Had never hung out socially outside of the occasional beer with other officers after work. But they'd shared a patrol car for two years, and they'd worked plenty of cases together since they both made detective.

Why would he think Rob was using?

"We found sleeping pills in your room. Your wife says you've been taking them for a few days, that you've been having trouble sleeping. Bad dreams. We also know you've been seeing a shrink."

"That's supposed to be confidential!" Rob started to stand up but Sloan waved him down.

"Relax, Detective. Your records are confidential. The label on the pill jar isn't. It has your doctor's name. All we did was look him up."

Goddamn pills! They hadn't helped him a damn bit, and now they were just digging the deeper hole for him.

"Yeah, I took a sleeping pill. One. That's not a crime. And they're not narcotics. I've been having nightmares. This case... it's been eating at me. I suppose none of you ever had that problem?"

Sloan and Woods had the decency to look away, their expressions evidence they'd had their share of sleepless nights lately.

Choi just stared at him, his face blank.

"Guilt can make it hard to sleep, too."

"I wasn't there!" Rob heard the frustration in his voice, cursed himself for letting the FBI agent get to him.

Choi shrugged. He was about to say more when a uniformed officer knocked on the door and opened it.

"Navarro's attorney is here."

Attorney? Rob frowned. He hadn't called—

Allison. Thank god!

"I think that's all I have to say for now." Rob stood up. "Unless I'm under arrest?"

Sloan and Choi exchanged glances, and Sloan shook his head. "But you are suspended, with pay, while we conduct the investigation."

Choi and Woods left the room. Rob started to follow but Sloan held up his hand.

"Hold on a second. I didn't want to do this, but I had no choice."

"Jesus, Chief. You really think I killed that girl? Or the others?" Rob realized his fists were clenched and opened them. Took a deep breath.

"No, but we can't ignore the evidence. And you're not helping yourself. No alibi for last night. Kicked out of your own goddamn house. Seeing a shrink. And you look like you just got off a three-day bender." Sloan shook his head. "Have you seen yourself lately?"

Rob's lips tightened but he couldn't deny the chief's words. He had seen himself, and he looked like he felt. Shitty.

"You said it yourself. I'm not sleeping and I've had some marital problems. How should I look?"

"Go home," Sloan said. "Take a shower. Get your act together. And make sure you keep your nose clean. You're the closest thing to a suspect we've had on this case, and I'll bet my left nut Agent Choi's going to have his eyes on you until something else turns up."

"Yeah. Thanks." Rob slipped past Sloan and went down the hall. Going through the pit, the two officers at their desks avoided looking at him. *Already persona non gratis. Bad news travels fast.*

His attorney, a tall, frighteningly thin woman with skin darker than anyone Rob had ever met, even back in Puerto Rico, greeted him with a subdued smile and a firm handshake.

"I'm Leeza Johnson-Styles, your union-appointed attorney. How about you and I get some coffee and discuss your case? You look like you could use a cup."

"I could use a whole pot," Rob said.

As they left the building, he spotted Agent Choi sitting in his car in front of the building.

It was no surprise when the black sedan pulled out right behind Johnson-Styles' SUV and followed them to the diner.

"Thank you for keeping the oni away last night. I'm sorry you got in trouble for it."

Rob's hand froze halfway to his mouth, his half-eaten brownie forgotten.

Up to that point, the evening had been going well. He'd done everything he could to be a model father. Showed up five minutes early, showered, dressed, and in clean clothes, his eyes fresh and clear, thanks to some Visine. To look at him, you'd never know he'd spent the night wandering town in a fugue, was living in a flea-bag motel, and had been interrogated for hours by the police.

His efforts had paid off, both with the kids and with Allison, especially since he brought flowers and apologized for putting them through so much. She'd actually hugged and kissed him, and whispered in his ear how much she loved him. And that it was bullshit for the police to use his personal problems against him in a murder investigation.

Who knew me becoming a suspect would make her more protective?

Dinner had been more subdued than normal,

the spectre of the latest death hanging over them, but by dessert he'd managed to get a few smiles from both Heather and Ken.

And then Ken stunned him with his statement.

"What... what do you mean?" Rob asked, vivid memories flashing through his head. *Standing in the room. Knife in his hand.*

"Last night. In my room. You were there to keep the oni away from us. It must have worked, because it went to someone else's house. Did you follow it? Is that why the police were looking for you?"

Before Rob could respond, Allison jumped in. "Your father was in your room last night?"

"Yes." Ken nodded. "He was searching for the oni."

Allison looked at Rob, her eyes narrowed and her lips pursed, fighting not to yell at him in front of the children. She took a deep breath and managed to speak in a soft tone, but her voice was cold as winter ice.

"Rob. Did you—?"

"No." He shook his head, praying his guilt didn't show on his face. "I was at the hotel all night."

"But I saw you." Ken glanced between them. "You had a silver spear and you said you would protect us, that the oni wouldn't come for us. Don't you remember?"

"A silver spear?" Heather turned on Ken, tears glistening in her eyes. "You were dreaming, stupid. Just like every night. At least this time you didn't wake everyone up."

"Heather. Don't talk to your brother like that."

"I'm sick of all this talk about monsters! Somebody is killing my friends and for all I know I'll be next!" She pushed away from the table with a violent shove that knocked over her empty glass. "And no one's doing anything about it!"

Now the tears came full force and she stormed down the hall to her room. The slam of her door made everyone jump, even though it was expected. A moment later, Ken got up and retreated to his room as well.

Allison stared at him from across the table. "Swear to me you weren't in his room."

"I swear." The lie came easier this time, and he allowed some of his own bitter anger to flavor the words. "I spent the night in that shitty motel, just like you wanted."

"So he was dreaming?"

Rob nodded. "Of course he was. Unless you believe that I found a magic spear and went monster hunting. I've had my issues the past few weeks but there's a big difference between sleepwalking in your own house and driving a car across town and breaking and entering."

Allison stared at him, her eyes searching his for any signs of deception. Finally, she sighed. Reached across the table and took his hand.

"You're right. And I certainly don't think you killed anyone. But that doesn't mean you can come back. Not yet. You need to work on whatever's wrong with you, if it's some kind of PTSD or just too much stress."

"I know. One good thing, though."

"What?"

"Ken had a dream but not a nightmare. Instead of a monster, he dreamed his father came to the rescue."

Allison's mouth twitched and a tiny smile broke through. "Leave it to you to make yourself the hero."

He smiled back, not saying anything. Now wasn't the time for more words.

After a few seconds, she sighed again. "Okay. Sorry I got so bitchy. The day after tomorrow is Ken's appointment with Dr. Ellinger. You can take him like usual, and then stay for dinner, if you want. I suppose you've earned it, seeing as you're the knight in shining armor."

"I will be delighted, m'lady," he replied, in his best Arthurian accent.

"All jokes aside, it does make them feel safer if you're here when they go to bed. Why don't you go check on Ken and I'll deal with Heather."

Rob nodded and went to Ken's door. Tapped on it.

"Hey, can I come in?"

"Sure."

Ken lay on his bed, staring at the ceiling.

"You okay? I know it's been a tough few days.

I'm sorry about that." Rob sat down on the edge of the bed.

"It didn't feel like a dream," Ken said.

Rob's guilt twisted in his guts like a knife. He'd spent almost his entire life just like Ken, believing the boogeyman was real. That his dreams were real. And the one time the boy hadn't been dreaming, it was Rob's task to convince him he had.

Lied to your wife. Now you're lying to your kid. Tell me again about father of the year.

"That happens. I've had dreams so real you think you're awake, and then you really wake up and discover what you thought was real was still the dream."

"Heather doesn't believe in the oni. No one does. But it's real. And it won't go away. Not ever."

"I know you think that now. But remember what Dr. Ellinger said. What we've said. Monsters aren't real. Sometimes... sometimes people tell us stories. Friends. Parents. Grandparents. Maybe to scare us into behaving better. Or maybe just for fun. And they know it's make believe. Those stories, though, they can get into your head. Become real. And then you start imagining things. The tail lights of a car outside seem like big red eyes looking in the window. Or the wind sounds like something moaning and growling. But there are no monsters. Not out there, and not in here."

Rob pointed at the closet, and then under the bed. He hoped his explanation would mollify Ken, or at least get him to consider how his imagination was getting the best of him.

"You're wrong. The oni is real. And it wants to eat us. You have to stop it before it's too late."

"The police will stop whoever's doing all these terrible things. That's what you have to trust. We always do." Another lie. Who knew if the killer would get caught before he decided to leave town and ply his bloody trade somewhere else?

Unless the killer lives here. How long have you really been sleepwalking, Rob?

No. It's not me. I would never do anything like that.

The terrified face of a little boy appeared, blood running from the side of his mouth. He whispered to Rob.

"Tell that to my corpse."

Chapter Eleven

KEN LAY AWAKE long after everyone else had fallen asleep. He'd been so sure he'd seen his father the other night, had spoken to him. Knowing his father had been watching over them, protecting them from the oni, had been what allowed him to go back to sleep, to get through the night without any bad dreams.

But the more he thought about it, the more it seemed like he had to have imagined it. After all, his father didn't even believe in the oni. How could he keep it away?

Which meant it was up to him. There had been twelve people in the house besides him and Heather. Five were already dead. If the oni killed one per night, it meant they only had a few days at most before it came for them. Even if it took breaks in between to kidnap more children.

The police had instituted a mandatory curfew at nine o'clock. But that wouldn't keep anyone safe. The oni could enter any house it wanted. Unless people protected themselves.

Something scratched against the side of the house, near his window. A tree? Or claws against the siding? Ken slid out of bed and grabbed the glass of salt water and vodka he'd hidden in the drawer of his nightstand. A shadow moved across the glass. A branch blowing in the breeze? He took a step forward then stopped as a red glow appeared outside. Twin circles, moving slowly across the darkened square.

Oni!

Ken raised the glass to his lips, prepared to fill his mouth. The lights grew brighter and then disappeared. When they didn't come back, Ken approached the window. Nothing moved outside. Somewhere, a car door slammed.

Was that what he'd seen? The tail lights of a car reflected in the glass?

His heart pounding, he set the water down and opened the window. Put his face to the screen so he could see down the street. A faint, unpleasant odor reached him. Oni? Or just fresh fertilizer in someone's flower bed?

He closed the window and got back under the covers.

But he didn't return the glass to the drawer.

Peter Harwood lay in the dark, staring at the ceiling and wishing he could just run away and start a new life.

Unlike many of his friends, Pete usually looked forward to bedtime each night. Living with three mean-tempered older brothers and an equally heavy-fisted father, lights out was the only time he felt safe. During the hours between waking and going to bed, he walked around in constant fear of getting roughed up by his brothers or punished by his father, an ex-Marine who ran the house like a boot camp. Douglas Harwood had rules for everything and precise times for meals, chores, and sleep. If you disobeyed, you suffered the penalty, which ranged from getting a slap to the head to a leather belt across your naked ass.

Since the night of Chrissy George's party, Pete hadn't been able to sleep or eat. His father still had no idea he'd been there. He'd given a story about spending the night at Steph's house, and after all the trouble went down with Chrissy's parents, that's where he'd gone. Luckily, the Joneses were ultra-cool and they promised not to tell Pete's father the truth. Hell, they hadn't even grounded Steph. As always, hanging around his friend's family made Pete hate his own home life even more.

Then all the crazy shit happened, with Chrissy and her family getting killed, and now Sherrie Roper, too. Between that and the kids disappearing, the police were talking to everyone who'd been at the party and Pete knew that sooner or later it would get back to his father that he'd been there and not at Steph's.

Then there'd be hell to pay.

Lying. Keeping secrets. Drinking.

How many lashes with the belt did that add up to? Fifteen? Thirty? He'd taken five the time he got caught with a pack of cigarettes. For two days he couldn't sit without leaving blood stains on his underwear.

This shit might put him in the hospital.

The ringing of the telephone shattered the silence. Pete's heart beat faster. He looked at the clock. Who'd be calling after midnight?

The sound cut off in the middle of the third ring. Not good. His father would be in a worse mood than usual when everyone's alarms went off at five a.m., complaining about his interrupted sleep.

"Peter!"

Oh, no. The fear living in Pete's stomach tripled in size, filling him with a dreadful certainty. This was it. Someone, probably the police, had just informed his father about the party. Now it was punishment time.

"Coming," he said, his voice cracking at the end. He briefly considered running out the front door and never coming back, but he knew that was useless. He'd get caught, brought home, and get double the punishment.

Take it like a man. His father's words, every time he

delivered a beating. *Once it's done, it's done.*

Still, his body refused to move. His arms and legs shook, and tears ran down his cheeks. He wanted to wipe them away—crying got you an extra lash—but his hands remained frozen in place.

Something crashed downstairs. Pete twitched but he remained seated. Another crash, this one louder, followed by a deep grunting noise. *What the hell is he doing?* Pete imagined his father so enraged he'd decided not to wait, he was coming upstairs and breaking all the furniture along the way.

As if to verify Pete's thought, a heavy thud echoed up, and then glass shattered. The violent noises grew worse. *Thump! Crack!* All accompanied by the grunting, almost growling sounds of his father's wrath.

Then everything went quiet.

Peter remained in place, his chest heaving, his blood pounding in his ears.

No. Not his blood. Footsteps. Heavy, deliberate footsteps coming up the stairs. *Clump. Clump. Clump.*

This is it. Pete bit his lip as tears flowed. *I wish I never went to that party. I wish—*

His door crashed open and he cried out at the sight of his father standing there, towering over him in the dim light, his head nearly touching the ceiling...

Wait. He's not that tall. How...?

His father's head fell to the floor, revealing the hideous face of the creature behind it. Pete tried to scream but only a tiny squeak escaped. His bladder released hot piss down his leg. The beast's red eyes brightened, filling the room with a hellish light. The stench of rotten eggs and old swamp water overwhelmed him and he vomited his dinner.

The monster lunged forward with a roar. Giant claws cut through air and flesh with equal ease, tearing open Pete's chest and stomach and scattering bone and guts across the room.

Pete's body, already dying, tumbled off the bed. In his final seconds, a silent plea echoed in his brain.

Daddy, I'm sorry it hurts please stop Daddy please don't-

Thump! Thump! Thump!

The monster is coming!

Thump! Thump!

Closer now. But where? Too dark to see. Outside? In the hall?

Thump!

The door! It's behind the door!

No! Daddy! Help me!

Thump! Thump!

Thump! Thump!

Rob opened his eyes to unfamiliar surroundings. *Thump! Thump!* Something pounding. The door! El Cuco is—

"Shut up in there, I'm tryin' to sleep!"

Another thump. He recognized it now. A fist striking cheap plaster. The next room over, someone hitting the wall. The alien landscape shifted. The yellowed paint and peeling wallpaper of his motel room surrounded him with familiar despair.

Just a dream. Just another goddamned dream.

At least this time he'd woken in his bed. He'd gone to sleep fearful of waking up in some stranger's room covered in...

Blood?

Sticky wet puddles of red decorated the sheets. More of it covered his hands. He looked to his left and sick dread roiled in his belly.

Next to him was a dead body, wrapped in a red-stained sheet. A wicked-looking knife protruded from the center of it.

Oh, Jesus. What did I do?

He sat up, and only then did he see the body wasn't the boy from his nightmare. It wasn't a person at all, just a pillow.

Relief swept through him. Not a corpse. He wasn't a killer.

Oh, yeah? Where'd the knife come from? And the blood?

Rob shuddered. Had he attacked someone? Killed an animal?

Calm down. You're not the killer. You know that. Some of those houses had alarms. Others had all the doors and windows locked. You couldn't have broken in, killed people, kidnapped children, without leaving evidence behind.

Unless I'm El Cuco.

Stop it! El Cuco doesn't exist. Neither does the oni. And you are not some mythical boogeyman.

Rob repeated the affirmation several times before his subconscious quieted. He got up, went into the bathroom. Looked in the mirror. Red eyes, yes, but just bloodshot, not filled with hellfire.

Maybe I really am going crazy. I sure as hell look the part.

After splashing water on his face and washing his hands, he returned to the bedroom, where the knife drew his gaze. A carving knife of some kind, with a simple, unmarked wooden handle. Bending down, he saw the brand, recognized it as a common one. It could have come from any of a hundred stores in town.

So where did I get it?

His pulse picked up again and he forced himself to take several long, deep breaths. In the Army, they'd been taught how to relax and center yourself, to concentrate on one thing with single-minded intensity.

Breathe in. Breathe out. Clear away all thoughts except for the job.

After a couple of minutes, his body began to relax. His heart slowed, and with the adrenaline leaving his system, his thought process grew clearer.

First things first. Get rid of the knife. The pillow would have to go, too. And the sheets. Hopefully, the blood hadn't soaked through to the mattress. Bundle everything up. In the morning, sneak some sheets from the cleaning woman's cart, or pick the lock on the supply closet. It'd be easy enough to do.

He looked around the room. The floor seemed clean, and it only took a few seconds to wipe the red smudges off both door knobs.

Finding a place to dispose of the linens wasn't as easy. The police had impounded his car. Without it, he had to carry everything in plain sight. Anyone seeing him would be instantly suspicious. And remember him later. So he kept to the shadows behind buildings until he found a dumpster a block away. He stuffed the incriminating bundle into a trash bag and retied it. The knife went down a sewer, like the last one.

Sirens howled to life in the distance, which brought his nightmare back to him. Another murder? There were plenty of other crimes the cops could be responding to, but something in his gut told him neither he nor the town would be that lucky.

He'd barely crawled back into his freshly-made bed when the half-expected knock came.

"Navarro. It's Woods and Choi. Get your ass up. We wanna talk to you."

"You never left the goddamned hotel. How'd you do it?" The tendons in Choi's neck stuck out and every muscle in his body seemed tense, like he was ready to leap over the table and attack.

The morning had been a dark, disturbing version of Groundhog Day, with Rob ending up in the same bleak interrogation room with Choi, Woods, and Chief Sloan. Only this time, they looked as frustrated as he felt. It didn't take long to find out why.

But I did leave. Twice. How did they not see me?

"Do what?" Rob was sure he knew the answer—there'd definitely been another murder, he just didn't know who yet—but he had to play dumb.

Woods slapped a series of pictures down on the table. Crime scene photos, a body torn to pieces, gutted like a deer. Rob looked at them and bit his lip, his stomach threatening to rise up. You didn't have to be a coroner to see there were pieces missing. Or that it was a teenage boy who'd been butchered like a pig.

The same boy I saw in my dream?

Another set of pictures showed a middle-aged man dressed in blue boxer shorts and a sleeveless t-shirt, the kind some of the older cops referred to as wife-beaters or trailer chic. He'd been disemboweled and his head removed.

"Nick Harwood, age fifty-two. Divorced. The boy is his son, Peter. Sixteen. Wanna guess who he's friends with?"

Peter Harwood. Rob recognized the name right away. Part of Heather's crowd. He'd never met the boy, but she'd said he'd been at Chrissy George's party.

Another one. That's four now, plus some of the parents.

"It wasn't me," Rob said. He leaned back and

slumped down in his chair, preparing himself for another long night of questions.

"We know that." Sloan didn't look at all embarrassed by the admission they'd had someone watching Rob's motel. "One of the neighbors called in a report of loud noises and screaming at just after two. Our officer reported you were still inside the motel when he got called to the Harwood's not long after."

"So why am I here? That rules me out as a suspect." Just after two? About twenty minutes before he woke up from his nightmare.

Coincidence?

"You're still one in my book," Choi said, and next to him Woods nodded. "This doesn't clear you for the others. You could have a partner."

"Or there could be a copycat," Woods added.

"Bullshit." Rob turned toward Sloan. "I've had enough of this. Either let me go or let me call my lawyer."

Choi slapped his hand on the photos. "Goddamn it, Navarro! Tell us what the hell is going on. Kids are dying."

"Don't you think I know that?" Rob shouted back. "My kids could be next! I want this bastard as much as you."

Choi stood up so fast his chair slid back. Sloan put out an arm, but the agent didn't lunge forward, just glared for a long second and then stormed out of the room.

Rob took a deep breath.

Watch yourself. You don't want to let something slip. Like seeing the murders in your dreams or talking about demons.

"Can I go?" he asked, his voice calmer.

"Yeah." Sloan nodded toward the door. It wasn't lost on Rob that the lack of evidence was somehow making them more suspicious rather than less.

I've got to start being more careful. Next time I go for one of my midnight strolls, I might wake up in the back of a squad car.

And maybe you should, his subconscious replied.

He had no answer for that.

CHAPTER TWELVE

"YOU SURPRISE ME, Mr. Navarro." Dr. Ellinger pointed his pen at Rob.

"I do?" Rob stared at the psychiatrist. "Why?"

"You've become the boogeyman."

Rob's stomach twisted and his body twitched. He'd considered the possibility, but never really believed it.

"So it's true." Rob felt no relief. If anything, the weight on his soul grew heavier, the gnawing in his chest grew stronger.

"Yes. In your mind, you believe you're the monster. I expected that once you understood how your past guilt and the stress of these murders was affecting you, the nightmares would end. Instead, you're incorporating these new deaths into your fantasy."

"Wait?" Rob's world spun around. "You mean,

you're not saying I killed these kids?"

"Of course not. It's just your subconscious guilt manifesting itself."

"No. That doesn't explain everything. How could I possibly know about those murders in my dreams? See their faces?"

Ellinger smiled. "You don't really know anything. You just think you do. Your brain is stitching together unrelated events, mixing facts and memories. You've seen all of your children's friends at one time or another. Just in passing, perhaps, or on social media. Too briefly to even register them consciously. But the mind never forgets. And now they're finding their way into your nightmares."

"What about the knives? The blood?"

"I'm not saying you didn't do things in your sleep. For all we know, you broke into a pet store and killed a bird. Or ransacked a butcher shop. But you haven't murdered anyone. Haven't kidnapped anyone. The logical part of your brain, the trained police officer part, knows this. You said it yourself. You couldn't have done those things and left no evidence. Years ago, a boy called you the devil and you accidentally killed him. Despite therapy, despite logic, that guilt still festers inside you. Now you're twisting it around with your childhood tales of a boogeyman and making yourself into the monster of your nightmares, because..."

Ellinger let the pause hang in the air, stared at Rob. The silence dragged on, long enough for Rob to become acutely aware of the musty air, the not-so-subtle halitosis emanating from the doctor's nose as he breathed.

"Because you don't want to own your mistake. To admit that what happened in Iraq was a result of a split-second reaction in a time of war, something that could have happened to anyone. In a way, it might have been better for you, mentally, if you'd suffered some kind of legal consequence. Since that didn't happen, you've been punishing yourself ever since."

Much as Rob didn't want to admit it, the explanation made sense. Way more than him developing a psychic bond with a serial killer, or transforming into a supernatural monster after midnight.

"So how do I change my subconscious?"

"You have to reprogram your brain."

"What?"

"Focus on two things." Ellinger held up two fingers. "First, Roberto Navarro is not a murderer. Not in Iraq, not in Rocky Point. Second, you are not crazy. Just an ordinary man dealing with a difficult situation."

Rob found himself smiling for the first time in days. "I thought you were going to say, there are no such things as monsters."

Ellinger shook his head. "Oh, no. There are definitely monsters in this world. Plenty of them. There's one right here in our town, killing innocent children."

"But not the boogeyman, right?"

This time it was Ellinger who smiled.

"Honestly, now. What do you think?"

Rob was just opening the door to his motel room when his phone beeped with a text message from Allison.

> Can u come over? Something u need to see.

Frowning, he texted back.

> On my way.

Allison was waiting in the living room when he arrived twenty minutes later. There were deep shadows under her eyes, and when she allowed him a brief hug, he smelled cigarette smoke in her hair and on her breath. That worried him. She'd given up smoking several years ago. If she'd started again, the stress must really be getting to her.

She stepped away from him and he asked what the problem was.

"See for yourself." She led him down the hall and pointed at Ken's closed door. "Go in."

Relieved that it didn't seem to be anything too serious—Allison certainly wasn't frantic—and more than a little curious, he opened the door.

A dozen snarling demons surrounded Ken.

Rob gasped and grabbed at the doorframe for support.

Hairy bodies. Mouths filled with sharp teeth. Eyes that burned like hot coals. A giant head atop massive shoulders. Clawed hands ready to rip flesh from bone.

El Cuco!

Then he realized he was staring at pieces of paper.

Pictures. Ken's drawing pictures of El Cuco?

Ken sat at his desk, his hand racing back and forth, creating yet another morbid depiction. His heart pounding, Rob stepped into the room, although the last thing he wanted to do was get any closer to Ken's lifelike artwork. The face of his nightmares leered at him from all over the desk and the floor and even the bed.

What in the hell is going on?

"Ken?" The boy didn't react. Rob watched as Ken put the finishing touches on another chilling picture, this one showing El Cuco breaking open a door. He set the picture aside and picked up a brown marker to start a new one.

"Ken." This time he said it louder. He waved his hand near the boy's face, afraid of touching him and possibly scaring him.

Ken's hand paused, and he slowly turned his head. His dull eyes and slack face made Rob wonder if his son was suffering his own version of sleepwalking.

"It's still out there," Ken said, his voice as empty of emotion as his expression.

A dart of fear shot up Rob's back. "What's out there?" he asked, even though he knew very well what Ken referred to.

"The oni." Ken pushed several drawings over. "I keep telling you. The game set it free. It won't stop until everyone at the party is dead."

"This is an oni?" Rob picked up one of the pictures, being careful not to let his fingers touch the actual drawing.

"Yes."

"Is this what you saw that night in your house?"

"No." Ken returned to his drawing. "I never saw the oni that night, only its eyes. This is what I see in my dreams."

A sharp intake of breath behind him made Rob turn. Allison stood there, one hand over her mouth. He shook his head at her, then looked back at Ken.

"Can I take some of these?"

Ken nodded, already focused on his ghoulish artwork again. Rob took the papers and retreated down the hall to the kitchen, Allison right behind him.

"He's been drawing them since this morning. He didn't come to the table for breakfast, and when I went in to check on him, that's when I saw...I thought he might stop after awhile, but when he didn't, I tried talking to him and he was so distant, like he was drugged or something. That's when I called you."

Rob nodded, only half listening as he spread the papers out on the table. Some of the drawings were indistinct, just vague shapes in darkness, with only the red eyes visible. Others depicted a shaggy, humanoid beast with wicked claws and teeth. One in particular jumped out at him, a monstrous face peering through a window, the fiery eyes and gaping mouth in clear detail as it stared menacingly at its intended victim.

For a moment, Rob was a boy again, cowering in his bed while El Cuco stared in at him.

"Rob? Should we call Doctor Ellinger?"

"Do you know what these are?" Rob asked, ignoring her question.

"He said they're those oni things, the demons he keeps talking about."

"They're not. At least, it's not only what they are."

"I don't understand." Allison picked one up and then quickly put it down again, rubbed her hand on her pants.

"It's El Cuco. The monster from my own nightmares. This is what I saw as a boy, what came after me every night in my dreams. This is what wakes me up screaming now."

"That's impossible. How could you be seeing the same thing? Didn't you once tell me that this cuckoo thing—"

"El Cuco."

"Whatever. That this Cuco is part of the Hispanic culture? That different islands have different versions of it?"

Rob nodded. Over the years, he'd done some research into the legends of El Cuco. Many of the Caribbean and Latin American countries had stories of El Cuco or Coco. Sometimes it appeared as a man with a pumpkin head. Other times it was a bear-like creature or a shadow in the night, the formless thing under the bed.

When Rob's grandmother spoke of it, she'd always described it as half man, half beast, just like the one he saw. Now he understood that she'd implanted that image in his young, impressionable brain.

But how had Ken come up with exactly the same fantasy? They'd never discussed the details of Rob's dreams in front of Ken or Heather, just that sometimes Daddy had nightmares and it was nothing to worry about.

It hit Rob that they'd never bothered to look up the oni on the internet. Maybe this was simply a case of two cultures having similar descriptions of monsters, the way so many countries had similar tales of vampires or werewolves.

"Go get the laptop," he said. "We need to figure this out."

Five minutes later, he had all the information he needed and a cold, squirming eel of fear in his belly.

Oni were Japanese demons, most frequently

described as troll-like monsters that appeared only in the night. Stories of oni were used to frighten children into doing homework or keeping their rooms clean.

"It's the Japanese boogeyman," Allison said, reading over his shoulder. A Wiki page showed a picture of a slant-eyed, furry man-thing dressed in a kimono, brandishing a massive club.

"Just like El Cuco."

Allison's hands rubbed his shoulders, which refused to relax. "That explains why the two look the same. Every culture has a boogeyman, and they're always big hairy monsters that live under the bed or in the closet. I heard stories like that when I was a kid, too. But it was from the kids at school, not my parents."

She sounded too happy, considering their situation, and he looked up at her. She saw his expression and smiled.

"Don't you get it? We've been telling Ken there's no such thing as oni, as monsters. But now he might believe us if he knows every kid grows up with boogeyman stories. That it's just a fairy tale invented to scare kids. And if we can't convince him, Dr. Ellinger can."

Rob nodded, although he wasn't as confident as Allison it would work. He'd been thinking just the opposite. A bright but troubled kid like Ken might consider it proof that the oni must exist, if people all over the world had legends about it. Still, they had to try.

"All right." He stood up, laptop in hand. "Let's give it a shot."

Chapter Thirteen

NEWS OF THE TWO murders at the Harwood home spread like wildfire through the town of Rocky Point. Bud Devins, father of Pete's friend Todd, had still been on the phone with Nick Harwood when the killer attacked.

"Most godawful thing I ever heard," he said, in a news clip that got repeated dozens of times on all the channels. By the next morning, it was on every newspaper's webpage, too. "We were talking. Nick said 'What was that?' and then there was all this growling, like a lion or something was there with him."

Pete's three brothers weren't much help. They'd heard lots of noise, but they just thought it was their father "beatin' up on Pete again." So they'd locked themselves in their rooms. The first they knew of their brother's and father's murders was when the police showed up.

Rob half-expected the news of Pete's death would send Ken back into his catatonic state, but the boy merely shook his head and pointed at the dozens of oni drawings he'd made.

"I told you. It wants to kill everyone from the party. Including me."

Unspoken was the fact that Heather had been at the party, too, but she didn't let it slip by.

"You mean us. Are you saying that psycho is gonna come after me, too?"

Ken looked up from his cereal. "Yes. The oni cannot be stopped. But we can save ourselves. I know how."

"There's no oni." Both Rob and Allison had repeated this to Ken several times the previous day, explaining that the idea of a boogeyman was something all kids believed when they were young, but they outgrew it. That they understood a human killer was a lot scarier to think about.

"You can't pretend it's a monster, though. It's just a very bad man who's doing very bad things."

Rob had even told Ken about El Cuco, and his own nightmares as a kid. As he'd expected, it hadn't helped. The boy still insisted the oni was real.

Now it seemed even Heather was starting to believe him.

She turned exhausted eyes at him. No one in the Navarro house had gotten much sleep. "Yeah? How can you be so sure? Monsters might not exist, but crazy people do. Maybe some sicko saw the same TV show as Steph and he thinks he's a demon who has to kill us all. And I might be next. He could be watching the house right now."

Rob saw Allison glance at the windows and he knew things were getting out of hand.

"Look. I'll call Chief Sloan. I'm sure they're already looking into that kind of idea, but I'll tell him anyhow. And I'll ask them to do extra patrols of our street." He might be *persona non gratis* at the station, but they'd do him that courtesy.

"I'd like it better if we went away until they catch the guy," Heather said, but she sounded calmer.

"It doesn't matter where you go, the oni will find you. We have to—"

Heather stood up and glared at Ken. "God, you are so not helping, you jerk." She stormed down the hall toward her room.

Rob raised an eyebrow at his wife. "Maybe I should go—"

"No. Give her a bit. Make the call.

"Okay." He dialed the number and got Sloan's voice mail. After leaving a message, he looked at Allison. "Now what?"

She shrugged. "Now we hope they catch the asshole very fast. Because if someone else—" she glanced at Ken and then back "if something else happens, we'll all be living in a hotel."

Ken listened to his parents and wondered how they

could be so blind. Cuco, oni, it was all the same thing. A demon. Until they believed, they would be in danger.

It's up to me.

But keeping himself safe and protecting the entire family-a family that didn't believe—were two different things. How would he convince them to do what they needed?

And then it came to him. He didn't have to.

And it was the story of Grandma Navarro that gave him the answer.

"We better not get in trouble."

Ellie Parsons lay on her back, Steph Jones' sleeping bag a soft barrier between her skin and the night-damp grass of Steph's backyard. A gentle breeze provided just the right amount of cooling, preventing sweat while never becoming chilly. Steph lay next to her, propped up on one elbow. Like her, he had his shirt off. Unlike her, he wasn't worried about his parents catching them.

"We won't," he said, running a hand from her breast down under the waistband of her sweat pants. They'd been making out for more than half an hour, and it seemed like they were about to get down and dirty.

"You're sure?" Excitement and nervousness warred inside her. She'd had two wine coolers and her body wanted release. Steph definitely had a shot at more than a blow job tonight. Maybe they'd even go all the way. She'd already gotten past her guilt of fooling around with Heather's crush. According to Steph, she'd been a real dud in the closet, even before all the shit went down.

Now the only thing holding her back was knowing his parents were asleep only a few dozen feet away.

What if they got caught? She'd ended up grounded for two weeks after Chrissy's party. Which wouldn't do at all, not when the hottest boy in your class approaches you in school and says he wants to hook up, that he'd have been better off partnering with you at the party instead of Heather.

No way she was letting that opportunity slip away. The hell with her parents, with Heather, and with Rick Garcia, who still hadn't gotten up the nerve to move past second base after three dates.

So she'd snuck out.

"Hell, yeah. My parents sleep like the dead. I've had parties out here and they didn't know."

"Well, then, what are we waiting for?" Ellie spread her legs and moaned as Steph's fingers started exploring. At the same time, he mashed his mouth against hers, his tongue a furious invader. An animalistic growling drowned out the sounds of the night birds and insects.

And then Steph was gone, replaced by a vile stench that filled her lungs until she couldn't breathe. Ellie rolled over, vomiting before she even got her head turned all the way. A gross mix of strawberry wine cooler and meatloaf splattered on the sleeping bag and her legs. When she finished, she turned to give Steph a piece of her mind. He must've lit off a stink bomb or something. Not funny. If he thought—

The deep growling sounded again and this time Ellie realized it wasn't Steph.

An animal? Does he have a dog?

She raised her head and a scream carved its way from her still-burning throat. A huge, hairy creature towered over her, Steph's limp body gripped in its claws. She screamed again as it bit into his neck. Something landed on the blanket—*oh god, his head, his head!*—and hot blood rained down on her. Steph's wide eyes pleaded for help that could never save him. His mouth opened and closed as if he didn't realize he was dead yet.

Steph's body fell across her, knocking her breath away and cutting her off in mid-shout. Panic overwhelmed logical thought and she beat at the headless corpse in a mad attempt to escape.

Pain erupted in her legs, red-hot daggers stabbing into her thighs. The beast roared, a primitive sound she felt in her chest and belly. And then she was rising up and up, feet first into the air. Her stomach rebelled and she vomited again. Bile and acid filled her nose and mouth. Blood rushed to her head and colored lights sparkled in her vision. She couldn't breathe, couldn't think.

The creature brought its face even with hers. Red orbs glowed like stoplights. It opened its enormous mouth, revealing a black cavern lined with jagged knives. The stench overwhelmed her and she squeezed her eyes shut.

The last thing she knew was the agony of her face being peeled away.

Inside the house, Zach and Emma Jones, deep in pot-induced sleep, never stirred until the police burst into their bedroom.

Ken lay awake in his bed long after everyone else fell asleep. It was only a matter of time before the oni showed up; if not tonight, then tomorrow. Or the next night. Six people were dead already. That meant less than a week at most, even if it saved them for last.

After dinner, he'd tried again to tell everyone how to ward off the oni, but they didn't want to hear it. They still believed a person was responsible, as if one man, or even several, could do what the oni had done.

"The police are watching our house," his father said. "And the houses of the other kids from the party. They'll catch this lunatic."

"You don't believe that," Ken had said. He'd seen the truth in his father's eyes. Some part of him believed the monster was real, but he couldn't admit it. Not to his family, not to himself. Ken didn't understand that. His father had confessed he used to have nightmares about his own oni, what he called El Cuco. And although he hadn't said it out loud, Ken was sure he was probably having them again, that's why he'd been having nightmares and sleepwalking.

At least his father hadn't gone back to the hotel. After saying goodnight and closing Ken's door, Ken had heard his mother ask him to stay, she'd feel safer with him home, and then they both went into their bedroom.

It won't matter if they don't believe.

That left Ken with no choice but to keep watch, because when the oni showed up, someone would have to drive it away. And no matter how terrified he was, he was that someone.

Just after midnight, his worst fears were confirmed.

He smelled it first, the all-too-familiar stink of decomposing food. Faint, just a tiny hint, like when a skunk passes through the yard and its odor drifts into the house.

Ken slid out from under the covers and picked up the glass of salt water and whiskey from under his bed. Similar glasses were hidden around the house. He'd snuck them into the bedrooms while the family was watching TV, and then after everyone was asleep, he finished the job, putting them in the downstairs rooms.

The rules from Hitori Kakurenbo said either

liquid would work. And according to his father, grandmother Navarro's stories said you should keep a glass of salt water under the bed to ward off El Cuco. He figured if it worked in the bedroom, why not every room?

To be safe, he'd used both ingredients.

Halfway to his door, he paused. Should he wake his parents? He had no idea where the oni would enter from. Downstairs? Heather's room? His own?

He turned and went to his window. Nothing moved outside. The oni was tall, but could it reach a second-floor window?

Glass shattered, the sound extra loud in the silent house. *Downstairs!* He had to wake everyone fast. He ran into the hall, shouting as loud as he could.

"Oni! The oni is here!"

The death-smell grew stronger as he neared the stairs. A thunderous roar announced the demon's presence, followed by the thud of heavy footsteps.

Gripping his glass with shaking hands, Ken continued to shout, shifting his gaze back and forth between the stairs and the hall. Thumps and voices told him everyone was up.

A vicious growl rumbled up from the living room. Ken moved closer to the stairs and looked down.

Glowing red eyes, large as eggs, stared up at him.

CHAPTER FOURTEEN

AT FIRST, ROB thought he'd tumbled into another nightmare, a lightless hell filled with screaming souls and baying demons.

Then he realized the sounds were real.

He sat up, trying to make sense of the pandemonium in the house. The sleeping pill he'd taken still wrapped his brain in fog. He swung his legs out of bed and the room spun around him. He pressed his hands to his ears. Too much happening. Ken shouting. Allison shaking him, calling his name. Something that sounded like a grizzly bear bellowing. An awful smell hit him, like driving past a dump on a hot summer day.

It's here. El Cuco.

No. That was his dream talking. Demons didn't —

Another roar shook the house. Heather

screamed.

"Rob! Rob! Do something!"

"Stay here." He sprinted for the hall and slammed his hip against the dresser. Bounced off and kept going. Pain and adrenaline helped clear his thoughts.

"The oni is here!" The cry came from Rob's left, by the stairs. At the end of the hall, Ken was a ghostly figure in the dim light.

"Dad!" Heather ran toward him from the other direction. He grabbed her and pushed her into his bedroom.

"Stay with your mother."

Without pausing to see if she listened, he joined Ken by the stairs. The bestial stink made it hard to breathe.

"What are you—"

"Oni!" Ken pointed down the steps. Rob looked, and his heart gave a painful stutter.

The creature of his nightmares, the beast that had haunted him since childhood, stared up at him. Its red eyes painted the walls with crimson hues and evil rumbled from its chest.

The demon let out a deafening roar, exposing teeth no living creature should have.

Rob reacted without thinking, clutching Ken by the arm and pulling him back down the hall.

"No!" Ken broke free and brought something to his mouth. Rob tried to grab him again but the boy dodged away.

And headed straight for the demon.

The next moments seemed to go by in slow motion for Rob. Lunging at his son. Something that smelled like whiskey spraying everywhere. Ken shouting in Japanese. "*Doko ka ni itte! Doko ka ni itte!*" El Cuco howling and snarling.

"Hurry!" Ken took his hand and pulled him away from the stairs. Together they ran for the master bedroom.

"Rob—"

"Daddy—"

"Move!" Rob herded them to the far side of the room. A heartbeat later the demon's pounding footsteps vibrated the floor and the door slammed open, lock broken. The demon's stench attacked them in foul waves.

Heather screamed and covered her face. Allison cried out and wrapped her arms around the children. Wedged into a corner between a nightstand and a window with his family, Rob tried to think past his terror. What could they do? They couldn't jump, not with a cement patio two stories below them.

We're going to die. Just like the other families. Torn apart, eaten—

"Do something!" Allison's hysterical shout made him turn. Her eyes went wide and she looked away. Rob's heart plummeted because he knew she'd seen the reality of their situation in his face and it stole her last hope.

Ken squirmed away from her and stuck his arms under the bed. Watching his son claw for imagined safety, Rob's despair grew worse. *We didn't believe him. Now he'll just die a second later than the rest of us, all because—*

"Īe!"

Ken stood up and threw something on them. The liquid seared his eyes like acid. He cried out and wiped at his face. More of it rained down, and he smelled whiskey, like in the hallway.

Another roar, louder and different from the others. Filled with a frustration and rage that Rob felt in the deepest, most primitive recesses of his brain. The bellow of a prehistoric carnivore deprived of its prey.

And then... nothing.

He opened his eyes. Through his tears he saw that the demon had disappeared. Unable to believe it, he stared at the doorway, waiting for El Cuco to return, to charge in and kill them all. It had to be a trick. The creature was playing with them.

The doorway remained empty.

"Is it gone?" Heather's trembling voice made him jump in the sudden quiet.

Before Rob could answer, a *crash!* sounded from downstairs and footsteps thudded on the floor. Heather shrieked and clutched at Allison.

It's back! I knew it was only—

A figure appeared in the doorway.

"Get the hell away from them, Navarro!"

It took twenty minutes to convince Detective Woods that Rob hadn't been threatening his own family. Even then, he didn't believe the story Rob and Allison told, that the killer had broken in and attacked them.

"This is such bullshit. Your son says it was a monster, and your daughter won't talk. The house looks like a bomb went off. I don't know what the hell is going on here, but you can't convince me you didn't do it. I was outside the whole time. No one came in or out."

"We were attacked," Rob said, for the tenth time. "I want that in the official report. The killer was here."

Even after Woods left, the crime scene officers spent another two hours combing the house with lights and taking samples from the rugs and floor.

By the time they finished, it was almost three in the morning. The moment the door shut, Rob gathered everyone in the kitchen.

"Ken, how did you drive El Cuco away?"

Ken told them about the alcohol and salt water, how it was supposed to repel both El Cuco and the oni. "You told me your grandmother kept salt water under the bed to guard against El Cuco. So I hid some in every room."

"Place a glass of salt water with an egg in it under your bed and El Cuco will not come in."

He remembered his *abuela's* words as if she'd said

them yesterday. Apparently, she'd been both right and wrong. El Cuco could come in, but it couldn't stand contact with it.

A pair of eyes, burning like hot coals in the night. Hairy arms reaching in for him, claws like a tiger's ready to stab him. Screaming. And Abuela rushing in. She'd comforted him —

No. Before that. She'd had something in her hand. Thrown it at the beast...driven it away.

Something in a glass.

Salt water?

Had she saved him that night? It dawned on him that he'd blocked out so much of that time, just like Ken had about his own encounter. Only Ken's had been much worse, and so his amnesia was, too.

He had no doubt now El Cuco had been outside his window that night. A monster that would have killed him in a most terrible way if his grandmother hadn't held on to her beliefs. And now the same kind of demon—call it an oni, El Cuco, or a bogeyman—was loose in Rocky Point, stealing children and killing people.

How twisted that only a few days after finally shedding his belief in the supernatural, he'd come face to face with the real thing.

Other facts Ken told them about the oni matched well with tales of El Cuco and the boogeyman. It only appeared at night. It ate or stole children. The Japanese legend of the boogeyman differed, though, in having a game to summon the demon into the world and then send it away. Just for fun.

Only the Japanese, Rob thought. Why in hell would anyone want to do that? More importantly, could it help them get rid of the oni forever?

"We need to tell the police the truth," Allison said, after Ken finished speaking.

"What are we going to tell them, a demon tried to kill us?" Rob shook his head. "They'll think we're crazy. Hell, they already think I am."

"They can protect us," she said, her voice betraying the fact that even she didn't believe it.

"They had a cop watching the house last night. How much good did that do?"

"Nothing can hurt the oni." Ken pointed at the empty glasses on the counter. "Even that is only temporary. It will keep coming back until one of us makes a mistake."

After that, there'd been mostly silence until the first rays of light ended El Cuco's nightly reign of terror. Rob sent Ken and Heather to bed, and after assuring them he'd be right down the hall, he returned to the kitchen. Allison had a fresh pot of coffee ready, and they sat down to discuss what they'd learned from Ken. When she took out a pack of cigarettes and lit one, he said nothing. Just handed her a dish to use as an ashtray.

"Okay. So here's what we know for sure. Salt water and alcohol drive El Cuco away, at least for a while. But it will come back the next night, if it's decided you're a target."

"It never came back to your house when you were young," Allison reminded him.

Rob shrugged. "I also didn't play a game that got interrupted. In some ways, the two stories, El Cuco and the oni, don't make sense. El Cuco chooses victims randomly, while the oni is summoned by the game and doesn't go away until you send it back or it kills all the participants."

"What if there are two of them?" Allison asked.

"What do you mean?"

"The murders and kidnappings started before the party."

Rob paused with his coffee halfway to his mouth.

"You're right. The timelines don't match. Is it two monsters, or did the party change something? Create a new pattern?"

"And how does it come and go at all?" Allison ran her hands through her hair. "Woods didn't see it. It just appeared in the house, and then disappeared. Where does it come from? Where did it go when it left?"

"Where did it go..." A discomforting thought came to Rob. Where *had* El Cuco gone after it left their house? "Allison, turn on the TV."

She flipped on the little TV on top of the fridge.

Ten seconds later, they had their answer.

Chapter Fifteen

THE POLICE SHOWED up less than two hours later. Rob and Allison had been waiting for them. Two children, each eight years old, missing from their rooms when their parents went to wake them for school. And Steph Jones and Ellie Parsons, butchered in the Jones' backyard.

"Police! Open the door now!" A heavy fist pounded on the door in accompaniment to Special Agent Choi's voice. When Rob opened it, Choi grabbed him, spun him around, and slammed him face-first into the wall. Before Rob could object, handcuffs closed painfully on his wrists.

"Stop it!" Allison shouted. "Leave him alone."

"Navarro, you screwed up this time. You're under arrest for the kidnapping of Melanie Peters and Julyne French."

"This is bullshit," Rob said, as Choi shoved him

out the door. "Allison. Call Leeza."

This time there was no interrogation. Rob was forced to hand over his personal items and shoes and then placed in a holding cell that stunk of sweat and fear. A heavy-set man covered in bushy hair and frighteningly realistic tattoos reclined on one of the two metal benches. He opened his eyes when the officers pushed Rob into the cell, and then closed them again when he perceived no threat.

Rob took a seat on the other bench, as far from the bearish man as possible.

The next two hours passed interminably slowly. The other occupant snored and grunted. Rob leaned against the cold cement wall, wondering what was taking Leeza so long. They'd have to tell her why he'd been arrested. There had to be something big; evidence, a witness, DNA. Chief Sloan wouldn't allow one of his detectives, even one under suspicion, to be brought in like a common criminal unless they had a good reason.

Which made Rob very nervous. He knew he hadn't been sleepwalking again; so what could they have possibly found?

He was beginning to worry that Allison hadn't gotten hold of Leeza when Chief Sloan and Agent Choi came down the hall.

"Let's go," Sloan said. His voice and eyes were both hard as steel. They didn't handcuff him, but Rob's anxiety didn't ease. Especially when he saw two more officers waiting at the end of the hall. The foursome escorted him to the interrogation room, where the officers stood by the door while Sloan and Choi took seats across from him.

"Anything you want to say?" Choi asked.

"Yeah." Rob controlled the urge to lean forward. That would just get him cuffed again. "Where's my lawyer?"

"On her way," Sloan said. "Meantime, this is your chance to make a statement. Tell us the truth."

"Truth about what? I was home all night. Woods was there, for Chrissake."

"Stop the goddamned charade." Choi crossed his arms. "We have evidence tying you to the crime scene."

"What evidence?" Rob asked. Sloan glanced at Choi, who shrugged.

"Footprints. Yours. Outside one of the windows at both houses."

Rob exhaled. He'd been worried they'd found something really damning. "Impossible. It wasn't me."

"Enough!" Choi slammed his fists on the desk. "Where are those kids, Navarro? What did you do with them? Tell us where they are so they don't die."

"I didn't kidnap anyone!" Rob shouted back. "And those footprints weren't mine."

"Do these look familiar?" Choi opened a folder and took out two photographs of shoe prints. The distinctive pattern of circles, lines, and ellipses identified them as sneaker treads.

Identical to the treads on the sneakers he'd been wearing only hours before.

"The prints on the left came from casts made at the Peters and French homes. The ones on the right came from the sneakers we took from you. They're an exact match."

Rob leaned back. His pulse thumped loudly in his ears and his stomach did a flip.

My shoes. At the crime scene. I was there. But I wasn't.

How could I be in two places at once?

The room dimmed and the voices of Choi and Sloan faded to distant whispers. His body was shrinking, shrinking—

Something struck his face and the world returned to normal.

"Navarro, are you with us?" Sloan was leaning over the desk, his expression somewhere between worry and hatred. Rob's cheek burned, and he realized he'd almost passed out and the chief had slapped him.

"It wasn't me," he said, but the doubt in his voice denied the words. "It couldn't be."

"This is getting us nowhere." Choi gave a disgusted frown. "Put this piece of shit back in his cell 'til his lawyer gets here."

The two officers lifted Rob from the chair. His legs barely supported him on the return trip, and when they locked him in, he collapsed onto the empty bench.

I was at the crime scene. I was home. I'm the monster. But

I saw the monster.

None of it seemed possible, but then, impossible was the basis of everything that had happened. To Ken, to him, to the victims in Rocky Point.

What if there really are two monsters? The other one, and me? That would explain how the murders started before the party.

He was still pondering that an hour later when Leeza Johnson showed up, an officer in tow, and told him they were going home.

"I made bail?" Rob asked, as the officer unlocked the cell.

"You were never arrested," she reminded him. "And you won't be, at least not today. Their evidence was bullshit. That's what took me so long."

"What?" Rob frowned. "They said the prints matched my sneakers."

"They were wrong." They'd reached the bullpen area of the station. Sloan and Choi were standing by the desk sergeant's window. Sloan held the bag with Rob's belongings, including his sneakers. Sloan's face was red with embarrassment, while Choi simply looked furious.

"It appears," the attorney said, raising her voice so the whole room heard, "Rocky Point's police and Assistant Special Agent Choi don't know how to read very well. The prints matched the brand and style of your sneakers. But they were also two sizes larger. And on top of that, there was no dirt or grass found on the shoes you were wearing."

No one said a word as Rob took the bag and followed Leeza outside. Dusk was already approaching, but the early evening sun still hurt his eyes after being inside all day. On the way home, Leeza told him that she'd already threatened the police and FBI with lawsuits for harassment, and that they "damn well better leave her client alone from now on unless they had real evidence."

"They won't," Rob said. "They believe it was me." He didn't add that he wasn't even sure himself if he was guilty.

"I know. But all they can do is monitor you. No different than what they've been doing. And as much as I hate to say it, to even think it, if there's another murder while they've got you under surveillance, that's all we'll need in court to prove you're innocent."

Rob thanked her and watched her drive off, wishing he could believe in his innocence as much as she did. Then he went inside.

There was a lot to do before nightfall.

"Help!"

Rob jumped up from the couch where he'd fallen asleep, a glass of whiskey on the floor within easy reach. The darkness turned the room into an unfamiliar maze filled with murky obstacles. He grabbed the glass as another scream echoed through the house.

Upstairs!

A woman's voice. Heather or Allison? It didn't matter. He ran for the stairs and found a dining room instead. He turned the other way. Stairs where the front door should be. Nothing made sense. It didn't matter. He had to save his family.

The bestial roar of El Cuco rocked the house. It was here! He ran up the steps, whiskey in hand. It had worked before. When Ken used it. Ken. Where was he?

At the landing, he looked left. A bathroom. In the wrong place. Looked right. A bedroom. The door open. Shadows inside.

He entered.

Cuco!

Blood dripped from its claws. The stench of rotten flesh poisoned the air. It towered over the couple on the bed. A man and a woman. Older. Gray. Dark skin against yellow sheets.

"Hey!" Rob shouted. El Cuco turned. Its red eyes burned with evil as Rob hurled the glass of whiskey at it.

The creature let out a triumphant bellow as the glass passed through it and disappeared. Long arms reached out, claws extended for a killing blow—

"No!"

Rob woke as he landed on the living room floor. His floor, his house. He sat up, squinting against the lights he'd left on. His hand found something cold and wet—*blood!*—no, only the glass of whiskey, fallen over and dampening the carpet.

Footsteps on the stairs. He stood, the half-empty glass in his hand.

"Rob?" Allison's voice. Quiet. Concerned but not frantic. "Everything okay? I thought I heard voices."

"Just me," he said, flopping back onto the couch as his legs went limp with relief. They were alright. El Cuco wasn't here. At least, not yet. "Sorry. Everything's fine. Go back to sleep."

"Like that will happen." She came the rest of the way down and sat next to him. "Nightmare?"

He nodded. "Yeah. I was in another house again. There was this elderly couple. El Cuco was about to attack them. Then it saw me and came after me. That's when I woke up."

"It saw you? Has that happened before?"

"Yes. Once, when I—" He stopped. He'd almost said when I woke up in Ken's room. She couldn't know about that night. Ever. "When I saw him with one of the other kids. I shouted at it and it looked at me. This time was different. I threw a glass of whiskey at it. Nothing happened, it just passed right through it. But it turned and came for me."

"Do you think you stopped it from...you know?" Both of them accepted as fact that he'd somehow seen another of El Cuco's visits, that it wasn't just a dream.

"I don't know." There'd been blood on its claws. Had it already killed someone else in that house? "I guess we'll find out soon." He got up and went to the window. Alan Woods' car was still parked out front. Another unmarked car idled down at the corner, where they'd have a view of the Navarro's back door. Choi wasn't taking any chances. "What time is it, anyhow?"

"Almost three," Allison said. "I'll put on coffee."

"Okay." There'd be no going back to sleep. Now it was just a matter of waiting.

They hadn't even finished their first cups when Rob's police radio crackled to life.

"All units respond. Ten-twenty-seven at four-eight-one Bower Place."

Rob shuddered. Violent crime call. All units meant it was a bad one. He looked at Allison.

"I'll call Leeza."

He was still reaching for the phone when Heather screamed from upstairs. Rob pounded up the stairs, knowing he'd be too late, El Cuco had her, had Ken.

Instead, he found her staring at her phone, tears streaming down her face.

"Heather! Thank god!" Allison pulled her tight.

"What happened?" Rob asked. The sudden relief at seeing her alive caused him to stumble. He'd been so sure...

Ken pointed at the phone. Rob took it from Heather's hand and read the text message.

> Cassie: Body's dead. The monster got him.

Chapter Sixteen

MORNING ARRIVED with rain and wind, a gloomy, dark day that mirrored the mood at Rocky Point High School. The news of Body White's death-and his parents'—was the only thing on everyone's minds and lips as they moved listlessly from class to class.

Students spoke in hushed somber tones about funeral arrangements and viewings, all the usual boisterousness of youth squashed by the spectre of death walking among them. Teachers reminded them about the school's counseling services and gave dispirited lectures that no one paid attention to.

At lunch, Heather sat with Cassie, Todd, and Rick. Cassie had started calling them the Final Four. When Heather reminded her that Ken's friend Jaime Black was still alive, Todd got pissed and told her to shut up, what did it matter? They were all doomed.

"Maybe they'll catch the guy," Cassie said. She lifted her sandwich, stared at it, put it down. She'd only taken one bite and a sip of soda. Heather hadn't even managed that. Her stomach was in knots and it only made things worse that she couldn't tell them the truth. The police would never catch the killer because it wasn't human.

She wished she could. She wanted to tell them that she'd seen the monster with her own eyes. That they needed to arm themselves with salt water and alcohol at night.

If Steph had known, maybe he'd still be alive. Ellie and Body, too. It's your fault, just like it will be your fault if anyone else dies.

Instead, she got up and ran out of the cafeteria, leaving her friend with her false hopes. Todd was right. They were all doomed. Even if she told them about El Cuco, they'd just laugh and call her crazy.

She ran to the first bathroom she came to and locked herself in a stall so she could cry without anyone seeing her. She'd barely sat down when it all came rushing out—her fear, her grief, her guilt—in giant, braying sobs. Her tears ran like rivers down her cheeks, turning black as they dissolved her mascara. Sharp pains stabbed at her chest and she doubled over, clutching her arms around herself.

It wasn't fair! Her friends were dead, Steph was dead, all because of a stupid game! She couldn't feel any anger that Steph and Ellie had been together. Yeah, they'd cheated on her, but they didn't deserve to die. Especially not like that.

The worst part was, they couldn't even leave, get out of town. According to Ken, you couldn't run away or hide from the boogeyman.

The bell for seventh period rang but Heather ignored it. She couldn't handle any more classes. Not today. And she doubted anyone would give her shit.

I'll go home. It's only a couple of hours early anyhow. And maybe Mom or Dad will have figured out a way to keep us safe tonight.

Decision made, she left the bathroom and ducked out a side door before she could change her mind. She'd never cut school before, and while this seemed like a damned good time to start, it still felt weird.

"Heather!"

She jumped at the sound of her name, her body reacting like she'd been caught by the teacher even as she recognized the voice.

Ken. Cutting across the school lawn.

"What are you doing?" she asked, as he caught up with her.

"The same thing as you," he said, with no trace of guilt. "I want to help Mom and Dad."

Heather didn't correct his assumption, but guilt weighed on her all the way home. She'd left because she was scared; her fourteen-year-old brother was acting out of bravery. Sure, he was frightened, too. But instead of being a coward, he wanted to help protect the family. She didn't know if that was a cultural thing or just who he was, but it made her both admire and resent him.

No, not resent. Admit it, you're jealous. He's a better person than you are. He's faced the demon twice already, once when he was only eight. Eight! And he saved all of us the other night, stood face-to-face with that thing and drove it away.

While you sat on the bed and screamed like a baby.

She glanced at Ken, who wore his usual somber face. If not for the heavy circles under his eyes and paler than usual skin, he could've just been walking home from school on any ordinary day.

For a moment, admiration won out over jealousy. She put her arm around him and gave him a hug.

"You're alright, you know that?"

He smiled, and guilt jabbed her again as she remembered how mean she'd been to him about Chrissy's party, and even before that. All the times she'd told him to go away while she was on the phone with her friends, or complained about having to take him to the mall or the comic book store.

Things will be different after this. I'll be nicer. I promise.

Then another thought rose up.

If we survive.

For the rest of the walk home, she had to fight not to cry and she was glad for the misty rain, because a few tears leaked out.

The last thing Rob wanted to do was leave Allison and the kids—he still couldn't believe they'd both cut school to come home and be together as a family—just to have an extra session with Dr. Ellinger. The therapy seemed ridiculous now that they knew El Cuco was real and he wasn't crazy.

But Leeza Johnson-Styles was adamant he should go, because of the accusations of violence against him. Besides, he'd had those sleepwalking episodes, which meant he might still present a danger to Allison and the kids. He'd promised her he'd do everything in his power to put an end to them, and if that meant some extra sessions with Ellinger, he was good with it.

As long as they were during the day.

Of course, talking to the doctor now brought up other problems. As in, how to respond when Ellinger said the monsters were only figments of his imagination.

"Hey, doc, I just spent the last couple of days being attacked by a make-believe creature, brought in for questioning by the police, and monster-proofing my house. Did you know whiskey and salt water can repel a boogeyman? My son taught us that, when he used them to chase it away and save our lives."

The latest visit from Choi and Sloan had been markedly different from the others. They hadn't even taken him to the station. In fact, behind Choi's belligerent attitude, Rob had sensed a different emotion: fear.

Fear that the murders and kidnappings would keep happening, yes, but behind that lurked an even bigger worry: that Rob might actually be telling the truth.

And the reason for that was all over the news and social media.

Body White's grandparents had survived the massacre that left their daughter, son-in-law, and grandson torn to pieces. Rob knew that was at least partly his doing, although he didn't say that to the police. But while the grandfather was still in shock and not speaking to anyone, even the doctors, the grandmother had told the police and the reporters everything she'd seen and heard.

"Tonton Macoute!" she'd shouted into the camera, when asked to describe the intruder. "Tonton Macoute!"

Rob had looked it up.

It was Haitian for boogeyman.

He was sure Choi and Sloan knew what it meant. It showed in their eyes, the set of their lips, the tightness of the muscles in their necks and shoulders. The realization that something way beyond their experience was occurring and they were in over their heads without a clue.

For a moment, he'd been sure Sloan was going to ask him about Ken's monster, about what really happened in the house two nights ago. But he didn't. He couldn't; his police training was too strong. No matter how much evidence got dumped in his lap, he'd never be able to believe in the supernatural until it bit his head off. The same with Choi, and Woods. Even Ellinger. They were products of a rational world where monsters didn't exist.

Hell, who can blame them? I was about ready to check myself into the looney bin.

Which brought him back to his current problem: what to tell Ellinger. If the doctor thought someone was so crazy they posed a threat to themself or others, legally he could have the patient committed to a psychiatric hospital for observation. So far, Ellinger was of the opinion Rob's sleepwalking was harmless.

But if I tell him I was brought in as a murder suspect, that my son and I chased the boogeyman out of our house, that I've woken up more than once with a bloody knife in my hand?

That might change his mind.

He went inside, still debating what to do even as Ellinger motioned for him to sit down.

"You look tired," Ellinger greeted him. He wore the exact same outfit as always. Rob wondered if the man ever changed clothes; that would explain the funky odor that always surrounded him. Allison was of the opinion the man was a widower and didn't know how to do wash.

"The last couple of days have been... unusual," Rob admitted.

"I've kept up with the latest murders and kidnappings," Ellinger said. Something in his voice, the way he held his pen over the paper, ready to write, informed Rob the psychiatrist knew about Rob's place on the suspect list.

Might as well go for broke.

"This is going to sound crazy, Doc..."

Forty-five minutes later, Rob left the office vowing to never return. He couldn't take the chance, not after what Ellinger had said.

"I'm worried about you, Rob. It sounds like your previously mild delusions are becoming more serious. Studies show that PTSD can evolve and eventually become too much for someone to handle. Cause a psychotic break. There's a real danger of suicide. I wonder if we shouldn't consider having you spend some time in a facility where you can be monitored twenty-four hours a day. As part of that, we can conduct some sleep studies, try some different medications in a controlled environment."

The *ding* of the timer ending the session saved Rob from further discussion. He agreed to think about it and have a decision when he returned in three days.

Allison would understand. If he was locked away, he couldn't protect them from El Cuco.

Not that you've done a great job so far. If it wasn't for Ken, you'd all be dead.

Things were different now, though. They were as prepared as possible. Whiskey and salt water everywhere. He'd even gotten Heather's old water pistols from the closet and filled those. He'd also dipped bullets into whiskey and loaded them in his personal gun, a Smith & Wesson snub-nose revolver. It only held six rounds, but he wasn't expecting to kill El Cuco, just slow it down so they could escape.

And then what? Be on the run for the rest of your lives?

That was something he and Allison had discussed, out of earshot from the kids. If you couldn't kill El Cuco, couldn't stop it, where did that leave them? They couldn't live like this for very long, spending their nights waiting for it to appear and their days exhausted.

"We'll beat it, somehow," he'd said. "There has to be something. It can be hurt, we know that. Which means it can be killed. We just have to figure out how."

When he arrived home and told Allison what happened, she immediately agreed with him. No more Ellinger, not for him, and not for Ken.

She also had an idea to share with him.

"What if we play the game again? Ken's game. Only this time, we beat it, according to the rules. Ken said that sends it away and it can't come back until you call it again."

Rob's hopes jumped for a moment, then plummeted back down.

"It won't work," he told her. "For two reasons.

First, it still has to finish the game the kids started, which means Heather, Ken, and the others have to die before it leaves. There's no reset. And second, it obviously can appear in our world even when the game isn't played. How else to explain what I experienced as a kid, or the disappearances here before they played?"

"But that doesn't make sense. If it can show up anywhere, anytime, why don't more people see it? Why aren't children disappearing all the time? Why aren't there bodies everywhere?"

"I don't know!" The words came out sharper than he intended. He lowered his voice. "I'm sorry. I'm just frustrated."

"It's okay." She wrapped her arms around him and he returned the hug, taking comfort from the feel of her warm softness pressed against his chest. It was hard to believe that just a few days ago they'd been sleeping in separate places, a wedge driven into their relationship by a creature that shouldn't even exist.

That's another one I owe you for, he thought. Almost ruining my marriage.

I will find you and kill you, he vowed. No matter how long it takes.

He held Allison tighter. He was not going to lose her. Or his children. El Cuco had to die.

With renewed determination, he kissed his wife and went to the computer. They still had several hours until night.

He wasn't going to waste them.

Chapter Seventeen

IT'S TOO QUIET.

Rob glanced at the clock. Just after midnight. The silence in the house felt unnatural. Like it had weight. An ominous sensation he'd experienced a few times while deployed in the Middle East, but never in his own home.

Ken and Heather were engrossed with their phones. *He's probably reading and she's probably on Chatbook or Instachat or whatever the latest social media craze is.* Their eyes flicked toward him as he got off the bed. Allison looked up from her magazine.

"I can't sit still. I'll be back in a sec."

The worry eased on their faces but didn't disappear. It wouldn't, not until the threat of El Cuco was gone forever.

And when would that be? He feared it might never happen.

They'd decided that all four of them should spend the night in Rob and Allison's room, armed with their liquid Cuco repellent. If El Cuco showed up, they could blast him back to wherever he came from.

But sitting on the bed with his family only amplified his anxiety. They couldn't turn on the TV because they needed to listen for El Cuco's presence. They only spoke sparingly, and in whispers.

So it was just sitting and waiting. Sitting and waiting.

With a growing feeling that *tonight was the night.*

He'd had it before. Twice on guard duty, while Taliban forces gathered in the hills outside the city. For days, there'd been underground chatter that an attack was coming, but no one knew when.

He'd known, though. He'd gotten that feeling, that creepy, spiders-on-the-neck cold tickle that told him *soon.* And he wasn't the only one. As the hours stretched on, it spread throughout camp. Mostly soldiers who'd been deployed for a while, whose primal senses were attuned to something most other people wouldn't notice.

And they'd been right. Both times, the bombings started before dawn came.

The third time had been when they entered that building, the one where the boy...

The knife plunging in... "Bala." The grenade that wasn't...

There'd been no way for them to know. And his danger-sense hadn't been wrong; they'd been ambushed less than an hour later. The whole thing had been a setup. Maybe even the boy, a dupe told to leap out at the soldiers, the ball hidden in his hands until it was too late...

Rob forced the memories away, surprised to find that this time there was no guilt clinging to them. Had he finally accepted it wasn't his fault? Or was it just taking a back seat to the fear of facing El Cuco again?

At the bottom of the stairs, he paused, squirt gun in one hand and glass of whiskey in the other. The silence seemed denser here. It reminded him that this was where El Cuco had appeared the last time.

As he stood there, faint sounds, the background noises you only heard in the dead of night, grew audible. The soft tick of the kitchen clock. The hum of the refrigerator. The muted beep-beep of a car being locked somewhere on the street.

Satisfied they were still alone, Rob made his way to the front window. The two unmarked police cars were still keeping vigil. With all the lights in the house on, the officers had a clear view of him. He let the curtain fall back.

Time to go back upstairs. Allison would be getting worried.

No, be honest. You're *getting worried.* The oppressive sensation hadn't eased like he'd hoped, despite assuring himself that nothing—

Something crashed upstairs. A scream, and then a chorus of them, followed by Allison's voice.

"Get away!"

"I'm coming!" Rob sprinted for the stairs. The roar of El Cuco drowned out his family's cries. He slammed into the hallway wall so hard a picture fell, and used the collision to turn without slowing down. The seaside-garbage summer-roadkill stench of the monster hit him before he reached the bedroom door. Ken shouted something and the beast bellowed in pain and fury. Rob reached the door and time stopped.

Allison on the floor, her eyes closed, a red welt on her forehead. Ken standing next to her, squirting salt water at El Cuco, which had a screaming Heather gripped in its massive paws.

The monster looked at Rob. He threw the whiskey glass at it and the creature dodged aside with a triumphant bellow. Smoke rose from its thick fur wherever Ken's salt water struck it.

El Cuco turned and stepped into the open closet. Instead of clothes and shoes, an impenetrable darkness lay beyond the doorway. El Cuco entered the magical abyss. Its body faded, and Heather's as well.

This was how the creature abducted the children! It would disappear into wherever and Heather would be gone.

He couldn't let that happen.

Rob ran and dove across the threshold just as El

Cuco and Heather disappeared. His hand found her ankle and he held tight. A tremendous force wrapped his body and pulled him forward. Allison's voice reached him from far away.

"Rob! No!"

Light and sound vanished, and he was falling.

Then he wasn't.

He lay on his stomach. The darkness was gone, replaced by a dim gray sky with no clouds, sun, or moon. Thick mists swirled around him, hiding the damp ground and turning whatever features existed into murky, vaguely familiar shapes.

Movement in the fog ahead of him brought his attention back to the now. His hand still gripped Heather's ankle. She was prone on the ground ahead of him. Before he could say her name, two glowing red eyes appeared in the mist.

Cuco!

Rob dropped the squirt gun and pulled out his revolver, never letting go of Heather. As El Cuco rose, he fired. Two shots, then four more, pulling the trigger until the cylinder clicked empty. The creature howled in pain and clutched its chest. Rob was certain it would attack, but it turned and ran, its massive form quickly lost in the vapors.

"Heather!"

"Dad?" She lifted her head. "Where?—"

He crawled up and pulled her close. She seemed

unharmed except for some bruises and scratches.

"I don't know. But we have to get the hell out of here." He stood and helped her up. The alien landscape extended in all directions. Once more, he was struck by the nebulous familiarity of the shapes on either side of the flat area where they'd landed. Some only twenty or thirty feet tall, others rising up like the buildings...

Downtown?

As soon as he thought it, the entire place became recognizable. A street, and not just any street. Main Street in Rocky Point. He led Heather across the damp ground toward the nearest building. Up close, he noticed immediate differences. The stone and brick were fouled with brown and ochre lichens and strange mosses sprouting miniature red berries. Wooden doors aged and rotting. No glass in the windows, just empty holes through which unwholesome odors wafted out.

Under their feet, all that remained of the sidewalks was cracked, broken cement. What had been four lanes of Main Street was now just a long, flat field, with traces of blacktop peeking through wet earth and dead, yellow grass.

The temperature was neither warm nor cold, clammy but not enough to cause shivers. The air smelled vaguely of swamp water and mildew, like the basement of a long-abandoned building.

Rob kept a firm grip on Heather's hand as they walked, his other hand holding the water gun ready.

The plastic toy gave him no comfort. They'd already seen it wouldn't stop El Cuco.

They'd gone half a block when Heather paused.

"What is it?" he asked, looking around. She pointed down at their feet.

Dark red splatters decorated the decayed sidewalk.

Blood.

It had to be El Cuco's. Maybe bullets couldn't kill it, but they definitely wounded it. Where was it going? To whatever cave or shelter it lived in? Or back to the real world, to finish what it had started?

As long as it lived, Ken and Allison were in danger.

He had to follow it, if only to return home.

"C'mon," he said to Heather. She nodded, her eyes wide but dull. He hoped she wasn't going into shock.

The blood trail led them two more blocks, never diminishing but not growing, either. Whatever damage he'd done, it wasn't immediately life-threatening. Which meant it'd still be dangerous when they found it.

Then the splatters stopped. Rob stepped in front of Heather and raised the squirt gun. Looked all around, alert for an ambush. When nothing happened, he checked the ground to the left and right. There! More droplets, this time leading toward the moldering stairs of a building. Another wave of familiarity struck him. He knew this place, or rather a version of it in the real world. But it refused to come to him.

"Up here," he whispered, pulling Heather along. As they got closer to the empty doorway, the omnipresent smell of mold and toadstools was joined by the all-too-familiar stench of El Cuco, a mix of garbage, decay, rotten eggs, and maggot-infested meat. The vile odor quickly grew so strong Rob's stomach threatened to erupt and he worried the air might actually be toxic. Three more steps and Heather gagged and doubled over, heaving up the remains of her dinner. That was it for Rob. His stomach let loose and he spewed its contents everywhere. Puke burned his throat and nose. When they both stopped retching, their shirts were stained and all he could smell or taste was his own vomit.

It was actually a relief from the miasma surrounding them.

He wiped his mouth and nose with his sleeve and they continued on. As they moved deeper into the space, the weak light from the windows no longer reached them. Rob reluctantly let go of Heather's hand so he could turn on his phone's flashlight. Heather did the same. He allowed himself a moment of amazement at the way teenage brains worked. Even while getting dragged off to another dimension by the goddamned boogeyman, she'd never lost her phone.

With more light, he was able to discern specific shapes. A fungus-encrusted rectangle that corresponded to a lobby desk. Several low, square shapes in a pattern that suggested chairs in a waiting area. And up ahead, a dark opening that in the normal world would be a short hallway leading to...

Elevators.

He slowed down as something almost like dèjá vu came over him. Suddenly everything was more than just familiar. He had been here, it was...*no, it can't be. Here?*

The final pieces fell into place.

It all made sense, in a crazy, impossible kind of way. Everything that had happened the past few weeks. The murders, the disappearances, his own mental issues. Even the random evidence linking him to the crimes.

He'd been manipulated the entire time.

"Goddamn it." He aimed his light at the hallway. It did little to cut the thick darkness. He didn't care. He didn't need the light. He knew exactly where he was going.

"Hold on to my shirt, Heather." He led them into the same kind of endless black that he'd seen in his own closet a short time ago. There was a dizzying sensation of weightlessness.

Then they stepped into the real world again.

And although Rob had never seen the room they stood in, he knew exactly where they were.

By the smell.

Chapter Eighteen

"ROB! NO!"

Allison watched from the floor, helpless to do anything as El Cuco disappeared into the closet and Rob dove in after them.

A second later, a breeze swept through the room and the inside of the closet returned to normal.

Ignoring the throbbing pain in her head where El Cuco had struck her, Allison got to her feet and staggered to the closet.

"Heather! Rob!" She pulled clothes and shoes aside until she reached the back wall. Pounded her fists against it.

Something crashed downstairs. *Rob!* She ran to the bedroom door, but Ken stopped her.

"Wait. What if it's El Cuco?"

Allison hesitated. Her husband and daughter might be down there, hurt, in need of help. But it might also be the monster, coming back to finish the job.

"Rob?" she called out. Ken came up next to her, still holding his squirt gun. Her heart nearly broke at the sight of him, her brave little warrior, his hands shaking, his face pale, but ready to defend her to the death.

"Police!" someone shouted. "Is everyone all right?"

Footsteps pounded in the hall and then up the stairs. Two uniformed officers rushed toward her, guns at the ready. When they saw Ken, one of them shouted, "Drop the weapon!"

"Hold your fire!" a voice called out, as Allison stepped in front of Ken. Chief Sloan appeared behind his men, with Choi and Woods in tow. Detective Woods reached past her and yanked the squirt gun from Ken's hands.

"Where's your husband?" Choi asked, as the officers moved through the upstairs, searching every room. Shouts of "Clear!" echoed through the house, telling Allison there were more police downstairs.

"El Cuco took him. And my sister," Ken blurted out.

"What?" Choi stared at Allison. "Don't try hiding him. We heard gunshots. Did he kidnap your daughter?"

"No!" The last of Allison's control unraveled. "He tried to save her. It took her! It took them both!"

She fell to her knees, her body wracked with uncontrollable sobs.

"Mrs. Navarro. Where the hell is your husband?"

"He went in there." Ken pointed at the closet. "They all did."

"All?" Sloan pushed Choi aside and knelt down in front of Ken. "Who is all?"

"El Cuco. It took Heather, and my dad went after it."

"This is getting us nowhere." Choi took out his phone. I want an APB on Robert Navarro. Possibly armed. He may have his daughter with him. Sixteen, her name is Heather. About five-five and one hundred-ten pounds, light brown hair. Suspect is to be treated with caution."

"He's not a suspect. He didn't do anything wrong." Allison pressed her hands to her face. They were gone, Rob and Heather were gone and—

"Bullshit. If you know where he is, you need to tell us. Your daughter is in danger and hiding a fugitive is a crime. You could go to jail, too."

"Allison." Sloan's voice was soft, calm. "Please. Help us. What happened?"

She looked up, her cheeks wet and her eyes burning. "We told you. That... that thing came back. It took Heather. We tried to stop it. Rob followed it into the closet and they all disappeared. You have to find them."

Sloan touched her face. "Did he do that to you?"

"Dammit, why won't you listen?" she shouted.

"Rob didn't do this. He didn't do any of it. Not tonight, not ever. It's not human. Bullets don't stop it. Nothing does."

"El Cuco took them," Ken said. Tears ran down his cheeks and his jaw trembled as he fought to keep from breaking down. Allison hugged him close but he kept talking to Sloan. "It took them, they're gone, they're never coming back. And I'll be next."

"Jesus. They're all crazy," Choi said. He stomped away, yelling orders to check the attic and basement if they hadn't already.

Woods sidled up to Sloan. "Chief, I think Choi's right. They both need a shrink."

Ken gasped and stood up. He pulled free of Allison's arms and went over to the closet. Sniffed the air.

"Ken? What is it, honey?" she asked. He turned toward her, his eyes wide, not with fear but with surprise.

"The smell. El Cuco. It's the same."

"The same as what?"

"Dr. Ellinger. I told dad he smelled like farts. That's what El Cuco smells like, but worse. I'll bet it lives there."

Allison got up and joined Ken. The air still held the rotten odor of the creature, but it had dissipated. With only traces remaining, it did smell like a particularly bad fart. Or old garbage. She'd only met Ellinger once, the day they interviewed him about taking Ken on as a patient. Rob had brought Ken after that because he always had an appointment the same day. She didn't remember any odd odors, but she'd also been more concerned about her son's state of mind.

Could Ken be right? If there was any chance...

But they couldn't let Sloan or Choi know.

She turned to Sloan. "Are you done with us? My son is in shock and this isn't helping. You should be out looking for my family."

"We are looking for them, you can be sure of that," Sloan said. "And we're going to need a full statement from the both of you later this morning. A real statement, not this monster crap, or I will get a court order for psychiatric evaluation."

Sloan left the bedroom with Woods in tow. Somewhere in the house, Choi shouted for everyone to move out.

Allison watched from the window until all the cars had pulled away and then turned to Ken.

"Are you sure about Dr. Ellinger?"

He nodded.

"Okay. Gather up all the salt water and whiskey. We're going to pay your doctor a visit."

As she loaded the car with bottles and two squirt guns, she prayed Ken was right. He had to be.

Because if he wasn't, Heather and Rob were gone forever.

By the time they arrived at Ellinger's office, Allison's

brain was telling her not to do this. Breaking into a doctor's office in the middle of the night because her son believed a monster lived there? The more she thought about it, the crazier it sounded. They could get arrested. Or at least she could. And then what would happen to Ken? Back into the foster system? Rob's brothers had moved back to Puerto Rico years ago, and she had no siblings.

This is insane, she thought, as she parked the car.

But she had to do it. Ken had been right about everything else so far—the existence of the boogeyman, how to protect themselves against it. Why it was after them.

She had to trust that he was right this time.

As they approached the entrance, she realized she had no idea what they'd do if the doors were locked. Break the glass and set off alarms?

The door was open.

Inside, the building was eerily silent. Their footsteps echoed off the tile floor and lobby walls, loud as fireworks in her ears. Every noise they made was amplified by the cavernous room. The ding of the elevator arriving became a fire bell; the whoosh of the sliding doors became the groan of a giant opening its maw. Ken's hand trembled in hers as they stepped inside the claustrophobic space and she wished they'd taken the stairs instead. The elevator doors closed and now it was a trap, they were locked inside like two mice and the monster had them right where it wanted, it really was a mouth and now it was swallowing them—

The doors opened and Allison leaped out, pulling Ken with her into a dimly lit alcove. The mouth closed behind them and she couldn't shake the feeling they'd escaped death. Again.

And exactly how did we get here? I didn't push any buttons.

"Which way?" she asked, when she had her breathing under control. Her pulse still pounded like she'd run a marathon. Between the darkness and not being there in over a month, her sense of direction was all messed up.

Ken pointed left. "Number five."

Unlike the lobby, the floors were carpeted. Their feet made no sound as they slowly approached Ellinger's office. A hint of light glowed behind the frosted glass window set in the single door. Allison let go of Ken's hand and they both raised their squirt guns. It didn't surprise her at all when the knob turned easily in her hand and the door swung open.

An unpleasant odor instantly greeted them. It wasn't overpowering, like the stench of El Cuco, but she definitely smelled it. And it was decidedly unpleasant. It brought back memories of when she used to work for the county's Health & Human Services Department, before she got pregnant with Heather. Part of her job involved visiting Section Eight apartment buildings to make sure the landlords were in compliance with all the codes. No matter which building it was, the halls always reeked of sweat, dirty clothes, unwashed bodies, and too many different kinds of cooking in a small space.

Ellinger's office reminded her of that, and also Ken's description of old farts.

They entered a small reception area, just a handful of cheap plastic chairs and a simple desk with a phone, a lamp, and a calendar. Tiny emergency lights set into the base molding provided the bare minimum visibility. Across the room was another door, also with a frosted window. Allison motioned for Ken to stay behind her as she approached it. He didn't listen; instead, he moved several feet to her right, like a cop on a TV show.

My brave son, the hero. If they survived this, she'd make sure he had anything in life he wanted.

The door to the inner office opened as easily as the others. This time, the foul exhalation hit them much harder. There was no mistaking the stench of El Cuco mixed in with the cheesy, rotten odors of garbage and flatulence.

Allison paused before going in. The office was darker; the only light came from beneath another door at the far end of the room, and from behind them. In between, everything was a twilight mystery. As her eyes adjusted, she made out the shapes of two oversized reclining chairs, and off to one side a large desk with books and papers on it. A room-length, floor-to-ceiling bookshelf occupied the wall behind the desk. A single lamp stood between the chairs. Dark curtains covered what she assumed were windows.

She felt on both sides of the door for a light switch but found nothing. Ken took out a small flashlight and played the light around the room, then stopped with it aimed at the floor near the other door, which Allison guessed was the bathroom and maybe a storage area. Rob had mentioned once he thought Ellinger must have a little kitchen back there, which explained the funky odor in the place. Probably reheating leftovers.

"Look," Ken whispered. She did. It took her a moment to see it.

Dark spots on the carpet. Blood?

The light under the backroom door went dark, then returned. Shadows! Someone—or something—was in there. Allison's hands shook as she lifted her squirt gun. This was it. She would—

"Drop the gun! Hands over your head!"

Chapter Nineteen

ALLISON DROPPED the squirt gun and raised her hands as she turned.

Sloan, Woods, and Choi stood in the doorway, guns in hand. Two uniformed officers waited behind them. Choi wore a smug grin.

"I told you they'd show up. Where's your husband?" he asked, while one of the officers pulled Allison's hands behind her back. The other yanked the toy gun away from Ken and took out a set of handcuffs.

"Hey!" Allison broke free from the officer and pulled Ken close. "He's just a kid. Leave him alone."

"Ease up," Sloan said, and the two cops backed away. "Allison, where's Robert? We know that's why you're here."

"We came here looking for him."

"El Cuco lives here," Ken said. "The monster

that took them."

"Kid, don't start that shit with me—" Something thumped in the back room and all five men whirled around, guns raised.

"Whoever's back there, come out slowly with your hands in the air," Sloan shouted. After a moment, the door swung open.

Rob walked out, his arms up, with Heather right behind him.

"Don't shoot," he said. "We're unarmed and need medical attention."

"Heather! Rob!" "Dad!" Allison's and Ken's cries of joy sounded in unison as they both rushed across the room. The four of them wrapped their arms around each other.

"I thought you were gone forever," Allison said into his chest.

"So did we," he answered.

"Mrs. Navarro, please take your son and daughter and step away." Sloan strode forward. "Robert Navarro, you're under arrest for murder and kidnapping. Anything—"

"He didn't kidnap me!" Heather parked herself in front of Sloan. "He saved me. That thing took me, and we were in some weird place that wasn't Earth, and Dad shot El Cuco and we followed the blood and it led us here."

"It's like an alternate universe," Rob said. "The buildings are falling apart, and there's no day, no night. Just gray. But I recognized this place, and that's when I knew."

"Dr. Ellinger is El Cuco," Ken said.

"That's right." Rob squeezed Ken's shoulder and looked at Allison. "I'm sorry. All of this is my fault."

"I knew it!" Choi pointed at him. "Thanks for the confession."

"I didn't kill anyone." Rob shook his head. "But their deaths are on my conscience. It was my nightmares that led El Cuco to Rocky Point. Then it started kidnapping children, and it posed as a psychologist to find others. I'll bet it gave a lot of kids nightmares on purpose so the school would recommend him. And then when Ken and Heather played that game... it marked all her friends for death. And us, too.

"Navarro, you are batshit crazy, but that won't help you. You're going away for life." Choi motioned for the cops to handcuff him.

"But, officer, he isn't crazy at all. Despite my best efforts to make him believe so."

Dr. Wallace Ellinger emerged from the back room. He looked exactly as Allison remembered him. About her height, five-nine. He wore tan Dockers, white sneakers, and a button-down shirt. Behind his glasses, bushy eyebrows begged to be groomed.

"Who the hell are you?" Choi turned his gun toward the doctor.

"He's El Cuco!" Ken shouted.

"It's been fun playing games with you all these

years, Robert." Ellinger smiled at Rob. "Pity they have to stop."

With a sound like cardboard tearing, Ellinger's face split apart down the middle. The rip continued down through his chest and a giant, hairy shape burst free as skin and clothes peeled away and fell to the ground with a wet splat. The beast expanded until it was nearly eight feet tall and wider than two men.

A horrific stench filled the room. Allison gagged and the officers covered their faces. El Cuco roared, exposing jagged teeth that shouldn't fit in its mouth. Red eyes glared with evil intelligence from within deep sockets. It raised its hands and oversized black talons sprang from the fingers like a cat's claws.

Choi fired his gun and that acted like a signal to the others. Rob dove to the floor and Allison pulled the kids back as Sloan, Woods, and the two officers joined in. The gunfire was deafening in the small space and the kids held their hands over their ears.

Unaffected by the bullets striking it, El Cuco charged the men. One swing of its arm sent a cop flying through the air, blood spraying in all directions from a gaping wound in his chest. The second officer went down a second later, his throat torn open so badly his head flopped all the way back.

El Cuco grabbed Woods, who cried out as the talons pierced his shoulder. Ken picked up one of the jars they'd brought and threw whiskey at the beast. It dropped the detective and backed up, growling and shaking its arms.

"Go away!" Ken shouted. "Doko ka ni itte!"

"More alcohol," Rob told them, as he grabbed Ken's squirt gun. From his knees, he sent stream after stream of rubbing alcohol at El Cuco. It roared again and held its massive hands in front of its face. Allison heard Rob curse. The squirt gun was empty. He tossed it away and scrambled on his hands and knees for the other one. El Cuco went after him but Choi fired again, right into its face. The bullets passed through like it was made of smoke. It grabbed a screaming Choi in both hands and lifted him up.

Faster than Allison could follow, it lunged forward and bit Choi's face off. The last of the FBI agent's air whooshed from his lungs through what used to be his mouth. El Cuco dropped him and focused its demon eyes on Allison and the kids.

No! She could not let it get them. She looked around for more whiskey, for anything.

And then remembered the cigarettes and matches in her pocket. She dug the matches out and lit the whole pack.

"Hey, Cuco!" she shouted. It paused. From six feet away, its death-stench was so bad her eyes watered. She threw the matches at it.

Blue flames raced across fur still wet with alcohol. Shrieking as the fire spread across its body, it turned and ran into the back room. The room turned black, the same impenetrable darkness that had filled their closet.

"You killed it!" A crying Heather hugged her mother.

"No," Ken said. "It's only hurt. It won't stop until the game is over."

"He's right." Rob put his hands on Allison's shoulders. His face was bruised and his sad eyes warned her what was coming.

"Don't do it," she told him. "We just got you back."

"I have to. This has to end." He gave each of them a fierce hug. "I love you all. But only I can do this."

Allison could only watch, tears running down her face, while he took ammunition clips from one of the dead officers and picked up one of the pistols. Then he grabbed the last squirt gun and a jar of whiskey.

"Please don't," she begged him. How could he do this? Leave them behind? He'd die there, he'd—

"I'll be fine. I came back once, I'll come back again. I promise."

"Swear it," she said. "Swear you won't die on me."

"I won't." He crossed his heart and gave her a kiss. Then he looked at Sloan, who'd been standing in stunned silence throughout.

"Don't let anything happen to them," Rob said.

Sloan shook his head. "I'm coming with you.

That thing... it has to be stopped. Two of us will have a better chance."

Rob nodded and handed him the squirt gun. Without another word, the two of them entered the endless black of El Cuco's portal.

From somewhere far away, gunshots sounded. The beast roared. Someone screamed.

The portal disappeared and there was only a room again.

Allison put her arms around Ken and Heather and waited. Woods joined them, clutching his wounded shoulder.

They were still waiting ten minutes later when the first police cars arrived outside the building.

By then, she knew Rob wasn't coming back. But she couldn't leave.

"You promised," she whispered. "Damn you, you promised."

Chapter Twenty

ALLISON STOOD with Ken and Heather and watched the waters of the Hudson River flow past on their way to the Atlantic some forty miles away. The morning sun warmed her shoulders but couldn't thaw the cold, empty place in her heart.

She didn't think anything ever would.

Two weeks since Rob followed El Cuco into the wherever, and he hadn't returned. There also hadn't been any new disappearances or murders.

She kept thinking about the shots they'd heard, and the cries of pain after. Had Rob killed it? Been killed? Was El Cuco merely recovering from its wounds and then it would come back to finish its sick game? Was Rob lying in some alien wasteland, hurt, dying, trying to find his way home?

She'd been unable to think of anything else since that night in Ellinger's office. When the police arrived, she'd told them the killer had been Ellinger all along. He'd tried to frame Rob. When she arrived at his office, the 2 officers and Choi were already dead. Sloan had rescued Rob and Heather before the man could kill them, and then he and Rob had gone after the man when he escaped.

With no evidence to contradict her statement, and with Alan Woods backing it up, they'd been sent home after promising to give full statements the next day.

"Don't give up hope," Woods told Allison in private. "They'll come back. You have to trust him."

She knew in her heart they wouldn't. And with each passing day, that terrible certainty grew.

It was Ken who reminded her that the *Hitori Kakurenbo* game still wasn't over, and until it was, their lives were in danger. So one night she and Alan Woods broke into the Georges' house and located the teddy bear from that night. That was an experience she never wanted to go through again. Prowling through the dark rooms, jumping at every sound, her nerves about to snap. Then she noticed a shape behind the toilet in the downstairs bathroom.

She'd grabbed it and stuffed it into a plastic bag; even the touch of its fur gave her the creeps. She and the kids had spent that night locked in her bedroom, the bear in the trunk of her car. Armed with whiskey and salt water, they'd waited for it to come for them, but the night had passed peacefully. As soon as the sun rose, they'd gathered what they needed and headed for a secluded spot along the river. They'd chosen that spot because Ken insisted it had to be running water, and she refused to let him do it in their own tub.

Allison took the bear from the bag and set it on the ground. Ken took a mouthful of rubbing alcohol and spit it on the bear. Heather did the same, and then Allison. After wiping the bitter taste from her tongue, she waited while Ken and Allison said the final words to the game.

"We win!"

She lit a pack of matches and dropped them on the bear. The alcohol caught fire, and then the bear's fur burned, turning black. The stink of melted plastic stung her nose, and for a moment she was sure she smelled the rotten odor of El Cuco. Then a breeze came and swept the smoke away.

"Fuck you, Cuco," she whispered, and kicked the bear off the bank. It sailed down into the water and floated away. She watched until she couldn't see it anymore, and then took her children by their hands and walked to the car.

We win.

No, we didn't, she thought. We lost. We lost a great man. But at least we ended it. Together.

Rob would've wanted it that way. And maybe, wherever he was, he knew. He felt the closure. She hoped so.

Better to think that than to think he gave his life for nothing.

That night, sleeping alone in her bed and without pills and booze for the first time since her husband vanished, Allison dreamed.

El Cuco, chasing her down a gray, empty street. Its bestial howls spurred her on. In one hand she carried a long knife and in the other a gun. The broken, crumbling road made it impossible to look at anything else or she might trip, and that would be the end of her. She needed to find a place to hide.

Hot, foul breath steamed the back of her neck. She dodged to one side and her foot caught on something. She fell, skinning her arms and knees. Rolled over, bringing the gun up, too late, too late, the beast towering over her—

"Mom!"

Allison woke to Ken shaking her. His face was pale and his eyes wide. She looked around. Weak sunlight filtered in through the windows. She was sitting on the floor in a tangle of sheets.

"It's okay, honey," she said, holding her hand out to him. "Mommy just had a nightmare.

Ken shook his head, and his lip quivered as he spoke.

"No. I saw it, too. It's alive. And Daddy is still chasing it."

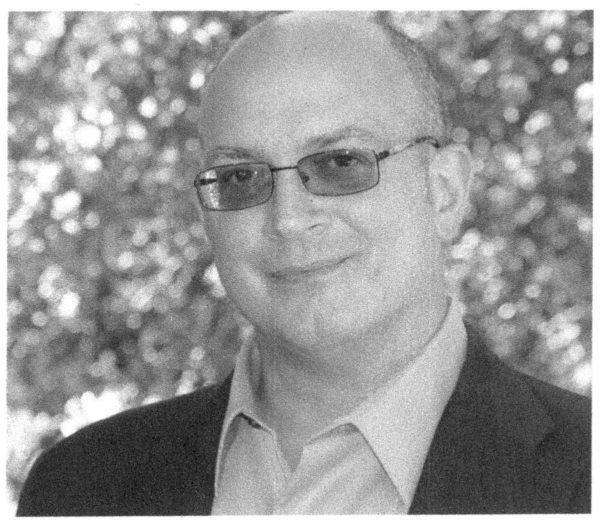

A life-long resident of New York's haunted Hudson Valley, JG Faherty is the author of 19 books and more than 85 short stories, and he's been a finalist for both the Bram Stoker Award (2x) and ITW Thriller Award. He writes adult and YA horror, science fiction, dark fantasy, and paranormal romance, and his works range from quiet, dark suspense to over-the-top comic gruesomeness. He is a frequent lecturer on horror and an instructor for local teen writing programs. He grew up enthralled with the horror movies and books of the 50s, 60s, 70s, and 80s, and as a child his favorite playground was a 17th-century cemetery, which many people feel explains a lot. His influences range from Mary Shelley (a distant relative!), Edgar Allan Poe, Jules Verne, and Tales from the Crypt comics to Stephen King, Karl Edward Wagner, and Alan Dean Foster. You can follow him at https://www.twitter.com/jgfaherty, https://www.facebook.com/jgfaherty, https://www.instragram.com/jgfaherty, and www.jgfaherty.com.

Milton Keynes UK
Ingram Content Group UK Ltd.
UKHW041616170724
445670UK00003B/36